UNSTOPPABLE FORCE

FORCE OF NATURE SERIES BOOK 5

KATHI S. BARTON

This is a work of fiction. Names, characters, places, and incidents are products of the author's imagination or are used fictitiously and are not to be construed as real. Any resemblance to actual events, locations, organizations, or person, living or dead, is entirely coincidental.

WCP

World Castle Publishing
Pensacola, Florida

Copyright © Kathi S. Barton 2013
ISBN: 9781939865205
First Edition World Castle Publishing April 5, 2013
http://www.worldcastlepublishing.com

Cover: Karen Fuller
Photos: Shutterstock
Editor: Brieanna Robertson

CHAPTER 1

Austin knew that if he laughed she'd come across the desk at him. He was bigger and much stronger than the fiery redhead practically vibrating with anger, but at the moment he was reasonably sure that she wouldn't care. But damn, he was thoroughly enjoying this. Maybe just a little too much. He wasn't a hundred percent sure what had pissed her off to begin with. He opened his mouth to bait her again when she spoke first.

"Look, buddy. I'm here because some asshole judge told me to be. I didn't realize that you had to have my pedigree to work here. I either work or go to jail. Right now, jail is sounding much better."

Austin looked down. It was either that or grin. He looked up at her and wiped his hand over his mouth, trying to stem the look on his face. "It says here your name is 'Lou' Cavanaugh. You don't look like a 'Lou' to me. What's it short for? I need it for tax purposes." She danced on her feet. "Why don't you sit down? This could be awhile since you're being so cooperative."

She looked at the chair behind her and then back at him. She didn't comment, neither did she sit. She'd been standing since she came in the room not five minutes ago. That's when he looked into her eyes. There was anger there, yes. A great deal of it. But he could see the pain now, etched along not only her eyes, but her mouth as well. He was just starting to stand when someone knocked on the door and entered.

"Austin, what is it?"

He glanced at CJ then at the girl.

"How's the interview going? Do we have another person to help out around the compound?"

Lou snorted. "Like I have a choice." It was low and probably wouldn't have been heard by any human, but he heard her. As did CJ. And CJ was in a better position to handle the girl than he was. He knew she was hurting and his first instinct was to help her.

"You'll learn respect here, Miss Cavanaugh. Or else you will go back to where you came from. I don't know your history, but we take care of those who work for—" CJ had been moving toward Lou and stopped suddenly. "You're bleeding."

That was the first time he'd seen fear in the girl's eyes. She took one step back then a second before she bumped into the chair. Her body language changed in that instant. She went from pissed off female to warrior female in a heartbeat.

"You mind your own fucking business. I came here because I was made to. Not to become friendly and certainly not to have you looking into my life." Lou turned to him. "Do I work here or go to jail?"

Austin glanced at his mate. She nodded slightly. Austin looked at Lou again. And he was surprised that he wasn't mad, upset yes, but not mad at her. He was more impressed than anything. He sat down, took out the sheets of paper, and handed one to her. "You work. Here's a map to the housing unit that you'll be staying in. Here is a list of times meals are served as well as a schedule. You'll be to work on time and ready. You'll do what you're told when you're told and how you're told to do it." He could see that she wanted to make a comment, but all she did was stretch her neck and nod. "This is the only chance you'll get at making any kind of comment on how badly you're hurt. If you can't do your job, now would be the time to tell us."

"I'll do it. Ninety days worth." He handed her the sheet of paper that was a contract that stated that she agreed with the rules and regulations of working for him. Without even reading it, she signed where he told her. She signed the paper "Lou." He handed her a copy. "Anything else?"

He wanted to ask her again what had happened, but only shook his head. Without a backward glance to CJ she left the room, closing the door softly behind her.

CJ sat in the chair Lou had never touched. "She's certainly something else. I've never seen anyone that mad before over coming here. Usually they are happy not to be in a cell for the duration. Why is she serving her community service here instead of the jail she seems to prefer?"

Austin leaned back in his chair and looked at his lovely mate and grinned. "George said he was worried she'd hurt one of the other inmates if they spoke to her. He said she seems to be..." He pulled out the fax from George Taylor, the county judge. "He seems to think she's ended up in his court room only because she had nowhere else to go. He also said he knows that she's basically a good kid, but has some trust issues. George thinks being around some of the pack will give her some of it back."

"Trust issues? I'd say yes, that's a fair estimate. But she is hurt. I'm not sure how badly, but she is hurt." Austin nodded. "Do you really think she'll hurt any of the ones in the house with her?"

"No. Not unless they try something first. She doesn't strike me as the social butterfly type." He handed her the thick file that had come to him yesterday. "This is what George sent me. He said it was thicker than this, but he took out the stuff that was petty."

Petty? He was amazed by what had happened to the girl and that she'd lived this long. First, there had been foster homes, then crimes that seemed to be more for her survival than anything else. He hadn't been surprised, however, to see that when she'd been arrested this time, she'd had no address or any sort of job.

"Austin, do you think she's going to show up to work or skip on us? We don't really need any more help on the projects. We're about finished with all but one house and Connor said he's doing that work on his own."

Austin nodded. They didn't need anything right now, but George had begged. He said that if Lou didn't get help now he was afraid the girl would get hurt or she'd hurt herself. He was afraid that she'd end up on the wrong side of a gun and he didn't want to see that happen. Not to this one.

"You ever see an animal that was caught in one of those traps? The kind where they chew off their own leg rather than wait for someone to come along and kill them?" Austin had nodded at George when he'd been in his office two days ago. "That girl is going to chew off her own leg."

Austin tried to think what he'd meant and looked up sharply when he thought he had it. "You think she'll kill herself?"

"Yes. Yes, I do. Poor girl has been on the run, mostly from herself I think, for nearly all her life. Her parents didn't want her, or so the records show. She'd been in nineteen foster homes by the time she'd been fifteen and had run off after the last one."

He started to ask why when the file had landed in his lap. "You read that. If you don't want to take her on then I'll understand. She'll be a handful."

And if the first interview with her was any indication, then he was sure she would be. He looked over at CJ when she cleared her throat.

"It says here that she was dumpster diving when an officer found her. She'd been caught before and warned off. This time she came before George. She should have been spending the next thirty days in jail for being a vagrant, but he sent her to us for ninety." She closed the file and sat up. "Why doesn't she have a regular job? She seems intelligent enough."

Austin didn't know. And for as much as he wanted to find out, he was reasonably sure that nothing from the girl would be forthcoming. He leaned back in his office chair and looked out the window to the woods beyond. He didn't look at his mate as he said what he had been thinking since her file had come to him. "No one wanted her from birth, I think. Her family, a married couple, had given her up just after she'd turned three. From all accounts her parents were the perfect couple. Money, education, as well as a nice little house in the 'burbs. I'm thinking that because they had enough money to grease a few palms she was put into foster care until she ran away. I guess she remembered her real name. Because she was dropped off as Louise Smith. By all accounts they didn't have time for a child." He looked at CJ. "Especially, I'm thinking, one like her."

"Like her? What do you mean? Is she not human?" CJ picked up the file again and began thumbing through it. He knew the moment that she found what he'd seen. "She's an empath."

Austin nodded. "She terrified her parents. I'm betting they paid for all kinds of doctors to 'fix' her and when that failed, they tossed her away. And according to George, someone is chasing her."

"For her abilities."

Austin nodded.

"And when they find her…oh Austin, when they find her, they'll hurt her."

He thought it would be worse than that, but didn't say so. He stood up and stretched. It was time to go find the foreman and tell him that he had a new hire coming on board and to tell him to be careful of her. Smiling, he wondered what Karl would say when he saw the girl. Karl Fitzpatrick was a large, loud Irishman who didn't know a stranger. If anyone could bring the girl around, he could.

~~~

Lou set her bag on the bed and sat carefully down on it too. She hadn't known what to expect, but this room was nowhere near what she had been used to. There were two beds in the room, both nice-sized doubles, two dressers, as well as two small walk-in closets. There was a bathroom that housed a shower, toilet, and a double sink.

Whoever had the messy bed next to her had already claimed the right half of the room as well as the right sink. Lou didn't care. She was here for three months and didn't plan on being buddies with anyone from here. Getting up, she took her bag and went to the bathroom.

Peeling off her pants, she looked at her leg. It was bleeding again. Taking the wrap off the wound, she hissed through the pain until the jagged yet stitched up cut was uncovered. Leaning down, she took a whiff and didn't smell any infection.

She'd hurt herself four days ago. Of course, had she not been running for her life she might not have hurt herself, but there was no help for it. When Dean Herman, a man from her past, had come up behind her, she'd hit him with the log she'd been carrying and took off. He'd nearly had her when she fell into the stream and got away. Dean screamed that he'd get her soon.

Taking out her small first aid kit that she'd put together over the years, she cut along the tiny stitches she'd put in the day before to take out the ones that hadn't broken. Using some of the liquid soap and a clean rag that she'd found somewhere, she washed the wound and patted it dry. Some of the stitches had been pulled loose and she needed to replace them. She had enough scars, she didn't need any more.

The thread was the normal kind that you'd find in any sewing store, but hers had been in someone's trash. She'd boiled it and then the spool. It was as clean as any one she'd find in a doctor's office, she figured. She threaded her only needle and took it and the thread to the sink to wash again.

It took her nearly ten minutes to replace the nineteen stitches and another five to clean her leg up again. Sweat poured off her forehead and along her back. Taking off her shirt, she rinsed it out and then put on the only other one she had. Taking the wet shirt to the bedroom area again, she was surprised to see that her roommate was on the bed.

"I'm Debbie Jones. It looks like we're going to be living together for awhile. What are you in for?" Lou ignored her and hung her shirt over the back of the headboard. "I guess you didn't hear me. I said—"

"I heard you." Lou sat on the bed and pulled out the map she'd been given. Looking up at the clock, she saw that she had eight minutes before she could leave this room to go to the mess hall. Standing up slowly, she moved toward the door, taking her bag with her.

"There's a closet you can leave your things in. No one will bother them. Not even me."

Lou walked to the door and noticed that in addition to the dressers, there was a laptop on the one she supposed was hers.

"You can use it all you want. They don't care. Just don't steal it. I've been keeping in touch with all my friends. Would you like to be on my list?"

"No," she said, then added a, "thanks." Lou walked out of the room and out of the building. She didn't have any friends and she certainly didn't want any. She was walking to the building that was marked on the map when she saw Mr. Force and his wife going in too.

Lou had been alone most of her life. The last ten years or so she'd been trying to survive. Not well, but she'd made it this far. Jobs were hard to come by without an address, and an address was harder to come by if you didn't have any money. She'd found that she could live on little and needed even less. The dining hall wasn't busy.

There were lots of things to choose from. Pizza and burgers as well as things like chicken and ham. Mashed potatoes as well as pasta were on the hot bar, and a salad bar was in the center of the big kitchen. Lou took a slice of bread and a very small salad of just lettuce to the table furthest away from everyone else and pulled out the bottle of water she'd picked up too. She was just finishing up her salad when someone sat beside her.

"How did you like your bunk?"

She didn't answer Mr. Force, but chewed her food slowly.

"Your roommate has been here awhile. I think her time is about up."

Lou drank the last of her water and started to stand. Mr. Force told her to sit down. She sat, but didn't look at him.

"You're not going to have any fun if you don't loosen up a little. Why don't you try to sit with some of the other workers instead of sitting all alone? Some of the people here are very nice."

"No, thank you." She started to stand again when he reached out toward her. She stepped back so quickly that she nearly tripped.

"I wasn't going to hurt you. I was trying to have a conversation with you. Sit down." She sat down, but further away from him. "Are you going to be this way the entire time you're here?"

Lou looked at the man. "Yes. Now if I have your permission, I'd like to leave now." She wasn't sure he'd let her, but he nodded. When she stood this time, he didn't make a move to touch her or to stop her. She was picking up her tray when he spoke again.

"No one will be able to get you here. You'll be safe." She looked at him sharply, then away. "Tell me who's trying to get to you and I'll make sure he never comes near you while you're here."

She wanted to laugh at him. She'd been made promises like that before. Plenty of times. Even by the man who even now was probably trying to figure out where she'd gone into hiding this time. Lou didn't believe this man any more than she did anyone else. Walking away without a word, she dumped her trash in the big can and put her tray on the top. She was out the door and into the night when she wiped the tears away. At least here for a few weeks, she'd be able to recuperate. She needed the time to heal.

Her leg was the worst of her wounds. There were a lot of smaller cuts on her back and on her torso. She'd been beaten pretty badly when she'd fallen in the stream and pulled downstream. So much so that she was reasonably sure she had a couple of cracked ribs. Then she'd been found and sent here.

She'd been trying to find a blanket or something she could clean up and use for padding when the cop had found her. He'd yelled at her a few weeks ago for digging through the trash. She never ate from the things she'd found there, but she had been tempted more than once. She usually raided kitchens or restaurants when no one was looking. And tried to get into a soup kitchen when one was open. But she figured there were more needy people than her. It wasn't the best way to survive, but it worked for her. Now, though, she was getting sick of it.

The room was empty when she returned. Lying down on the bed, she thought about how she'd ended up here. The judge, Judge Taylor, had told her he was doing this for her own good. He said that she might be able to learn a trade working on the Force Compound, as well as get a few meals. She wasn't going to be here long enough to learn much, but she was going to stash some food if she could. As soon as someone turned their back she was out of here. Closing her eyes, Lou started to count sheep. It didn't work very often, but today she was exhausted and fell asleep quickly.

CHAPTER 2

Karl watched the girl struggle with the boxes of tile. His alpha had told him to work the girl hard and then to see if she asked for help. He glanced at his watch and decided that it might be a long wait if he had to wait on her to give it up and ask. The girl was ten kinds of stubborn. Reminded him of someone else in this pack.

"You gonna let me carry that for you?" That was another thing about her, she didn't talk much. He could hardly get his daughter to shut up. This kid, about the same age as his own kid, didn't say hardly anything. "It won't be nothing for you to ask for someone to tote it for you."

The box had to have weighed around fifty pounds. The tile that was to cover the kitchen floor in this house was twelve inches by twelve. She put it down near the other five she'd already moved. She was supposed to tile this entire room by the end of the week. He looked at the size of the area again and thought she'd be lucky to get half finished. Then he looked at her. Nah, she'd get it done. He figured she'd have it done in about three days. Too damned stubborn not to.

The mud, or what was tile cement, had been spread about ten minutes prior to the tile being delivered. The girl had done a damned fine job of it too. He watched her open the first box and put out the large ceramic piece on the line she'd made to plum up the floor. Then when she started to put the spacers in, he left her to it. She'd have to ask for help soon or she'd be dead on her feet in a few days time. Grinning, he was amazed at how badly he wanted her to finish the room without a lick of help from anyone else. It would be something he could crow about, he figured.

Karl wasn't surprised when his alpha was standing in the room he'd been working in only moments before. He smiled when he saw the man pace. It was something he'd noticed he did when he was frustrated. Glancing back at the kitchen, he figured she was a great deal of his need to pace. Karl had been told that this girl was needing of some watching. Well, he could do that for him.

"She working out for us?"

Karl didn't ask who. The girl was the only new hire he'd had in months.

"She didn't have anything listed on her paper to indicate she ever worked on a site before."

"She said she could lay tile." What she'd done was point at it and said I can do that. "She seems to have a handle on it. Don't talk much, does she?"

"No, she doesn't. George was hoping we could learn a little about her. Maybe who was trying to hurt her? She didn't say anything in our meeting yesterday, but I think she's hurt. CJ noticed it too."

Karl looked back to the room where Lou was working again. "She ain't acting like she's hurt. But I know she is. Can smell it on her like some bad blood. Might need a closer look at it by the doc before long. She's a mite on the touchy side, but we'll...hell alpha, she's acting more like she's pissed at the world. You think someone tried to hurt her? Or you think she's hurt herself?"

Austin shrugged. "We don't know for sure. George says she's a good kid, just lost. I tried to tell her at dinner last night she'd be safe here, but she won't listen to me."

Karl guessed that's what had him frustrated. He knew the man to be kindhearted yet fierce. He also knew him to be slow to judge, but swift to make someone pay for crimes they might commit. This girl must be driving him insane.

"I'll keep her busy. She's only just started working. By lunch she'll be begging for someone to come talk to her and to help her. You mark my words." Karl watched the big alpha move out. Karl nodded again and started on the wall he'd been working on since yesterday. Hanging drywall was a younger man's work, but he was up for it.

By lunch, he was starving. He'd been working so hard toward getting the last wall in this room hung that he'd completely forgotten about Lou. Putting his tools away he went to the doorway where she was and stopped dead in his tracks. Holy shit, she'd been busy.

The six boxes that had been near her when he'd left the room over four hours ago were empty. As were five more laying beside them. All of them were neatly broken down and laying flat against the wall. She was nearly finished with the first half of the floor. He looked around in amazement. All that was left was the last three or four blocks in the row she was working on then the grout between the tiles. And it was as straight as an arrow too. Karl watched her put another square in place.

"It's time for lunch." His voice cracked as he spoke. "You gonna be able to leave that until after?"

She pulled a large piece of plastic over where she'd been working and stood. He noticed that she moved like she hurt now. Slow and easy, and she favored her left leg more'n the other. He thought about what Austin had told him and wondered how she'd come to be hurting that badly. Looking over the floor, he thought if she was, then he'd hate to see what she could do when she was at full strength.

Without a word she limped past him to the hall and toward the door. She left the house they were working on and off the porch. Karl frowned and shook his head. He wasn't sure if he wanted her to talk. He had a feeling she had a story to tell and it wouldn't be one of happily ever after. Following her out he watched her move. Yes sir, she was hurting all right. Her leg, he decided, as well as her ribs. She moved like a girl who'd been beat to crap and back. Karl detoured to the office and called Austin.

"You should hop on over and see the kitchen. That girl can work my crew any time she wants. Damned fine job she did for me." He smiled when Austin started asking ninety questions a minute. First and foremost was if she asked for help.

"Nope. Did it by her lonesomes, she did. And before you ask, she didn't say a single word. Don't even remember seeing one of the music gadgets either. She must have been in some kind of zone 'cause she nearly finished with half that floor." Austin asked where she was now and he told her he'd sent her to lunch.

By the time Karl made it to the dining hall she was there. He hadn't seen her at first, but finally found her in the very back of the room sitting by her lonesome at one of the long tables. He figured it was by design rather than no one wanting to sit with her. Karl decided that he'd respect her privacy and let her be. But Austin and CJ coming in made him think the girl wasn't going to be eating alone much longer.

Karl watched them go to the table. He knew the moment she saw them and watched her entire body stiffen. He pulled himself out of line to watch this. He had a feeling this was going to be fun.

CJ sat first. If Karl was honest with himself, he was about half in love with the alpha person. She was kind yet firm, and could be as gentle as a lamb one minute and tough as nails the next. Lou got up the moment Austin sat down. He couldn't hear what was being said, they were too far away and the noise level was too loud, but he could imagine. Especially when Lou sat down again.

When Karl's belly protested him not eating he sighed. He was going to have to eat and get back to work. Whatever happened here wasn't going to feed him. Taking his place in line, Karl kept an eye on the table and the three sitting there. He kind of felt sorry for the alphas. It looked to him like Lou was winning this one.

~~~

"It's a simple enough question. Where did you learn to lay tile? Karl said you did a spectacular job."

Lou fisted her hands under the table and didn't answer Mrs. Force.

"Lou, I would like it if you looked at me when I speak."

Lou turned her head and stared at her. Most people looked away, not wanting to make such a deep connection. She had to hand it to her, the woman was stubborn too. But Lou knew how to play this game. Mrs. Force looked away before Lou did. For some reason she didn't feel triumphant, only a little childish.

"Answer her." The voice was hard, compelling. Lou looked at Mr. Force and fought the need to speak. When he repeated the command, Lou did stand then and picked up her tray.

"I would like for you to call the judge. I'm done here. I'd like to finish up my sentence in the cell." She moved toward the door and out. Going back to the house, she was finishing up when she felt someone come in behind her. Not bothering to look up, she had an idea who it was.

"You signed a contract with me and I expect you to fulfill it." Mr. Force's voice echoed in the empty room. She hoped that he'd leave, but he stood there for several more minutes before he spoke again. "Karl said you could be on his crew any time you wanted. And he's right, you did a fine job on this floor. Thank you."

When Lou turned around he was gone. She laid the next tile and stood to mix the grout to get a start on that. She had to grab the wall when the shooting pain in her leg took her breath away. Looking down, she could see where blood had seeped through her pants. Picking up her bag, she went to the bathroom to clean up.

After she had inspected the wound, she sat on the toilet and wondered what to do now. It was infected. After all she'd done to prevent it, it was seeping yellow pus. She knew that this morning in the shower that it wasn't doing well. Frustrated because she'd done all she'd been able to do, she wrapped it back up and took two expired aspirin that she'd found somewhere. Limping back out to the kitchen, she began getting ready to grout.

The chills started about halfway into the job. By the time Karl had told her it was quitting time she was sweating. Walking to the place she'd been assigned to sleep, she couldn't remember how she'd gotten there. Lying on the bed, she closed her eyes and had to suddenly get up and go to the bathroom. She was sick. And after throwing up everything she had in her belly, she went back to bed and tried to get warm again.

Lou heard Debbie come in later that night. She might have asked her something, but didn't remember answering her.

When the lights were turned out and she was sure that Debbie was asleep Lou got up and moved to the door to outside. Burning up again, she nearly cried in relief when the chilled air touched her bare skin. She moved beyond the steps, not caring where she was going.

Some things in the forest frightened her. She saw trees that reminded her of her foster father and shapes on the ground that she thought were snakes and spiders. Moving along the trees for support Lou thought she saw a big dog, but didn't know for sure.

Sliding down the big tree she'd been standing next to, Lou looked around her. She had no idea where she was and while she had a vague idea how she'd gotten here, she wasn't altogether sure she could get herself back home. Shivering again, she tried to curl into a ball for warmth. That's when she saw the big wolf.

"Are you going to kill me?" He cocked his head at her but didn't come closer. "I wish you would. I've never amounted to anything and probably never will. That's what the woman at the last foster home said to me. 'Ginger Louise, you're nothing but a pathetic mess. You'll be lucky if you make it past your eighteenth birthday.' Showed her, didn't I?"

The wolf lay down on the ground, but didn't come any closer. Lou closed her eyes and tried to will the pain to go away. She spoke to the wolf as tears rolled down her cheek.

"I know what you are and that you don't normally… If I die out here, would you please not eat on me until you're sure I'm dead? I don't want to wake up and you're chewing my arm off." The wolf growled low and she looked at him. "I want to die. Just be gone from this world."

He sat up and looked to his right. Lou looked too, but didn't see anything until the moon appeared from behind some thick clouds. Eyes. Lots of them too. She looked back at the wolf and saw that his eyes were glowing too. She watched him as he moved toward her slowly.

"I want you to make it quick, please." She leaned her head back, exposing her neck for him. "Just take out my throat and kill me."

Lou felt him touch her foot. His nose was cold and she moved her legs wider to give him all the room he needed. When his hot breath touched her thigh, Lou moaned. She had no idea that pending death could be so erotic. Fisting her hands beneath her thighs, she waited for him to do it.

When his tongue licked along her skin, she opened her eyes and looked at the other wolves standing close. The wolf at her throat looked at them as well. His fangs bared then she heard a low, very vicious growl. Two of the closest wolves backed up.

"Please. I'm begging you, just kill me." He turned back to her and she could see his eyes. They were beautiful. A warm dark brown that made her heart pound. Shaking her head slightly, she grabbed the fur on his chest. "Do it, damn it. What the fuck are you waiting for?" Lou shook him then and he growled again. "Kill me."

Pain, nearly blinding pain made her vision swim. Her head had felt as if it had exploded. Lou looked up and then closed her eyes quickly. A man was standing next to her. When she tried to get away, back away, pain hit her again, this time in her leg. Crying out, Lou begged once more for him to kill her, but the big wolf was gone.

Closing her eyes, she sobbed. "Why? Why didn't you make it quick?"

CHAPTER 3

Connor watched the woman sleep. She'd been laying there for over nine hours without moving so much as her fingers. He wondered how much longer when he heard someone at the door. He turned to see Holly, his sister, there. She waddled in and sat heavily in the chair. Her pregnancy made him both smile and scared.

"She all right?"

He shook his head.

"Clint said that she might be here for a week or more. He said he'd never seen an infection spread so quickly in a human before."

"She's malnourished. He told me that had she been well fed and healthier, she'd be up and about by now." He looked over at her. "She wanted me to kill her."

"Austin told me. He said that you'd been helping look for her. It was a good thing one of us found her rather than a wild wolf. One of them might have taken what she was offering."

Connor felt the low growl come up from his chest before he could stop it.

"He also said she was your mate."

Connor nodded as he spoke to his sister. "So he thinks. I think she would have offered her throat to anyone because of her leg. She had five cracked ribs too, as well as a great many bruises all over her body. I wish that Phil were here. He'd have her healed by now."

Connor had brought her to the clinic by himself. Austin had offered to help carry her, but he'd told him to back off. The twenty minute walk had made him think all sorts of things and not the least of those thoughts was the fact that she'd wanted him to kill her. And when he'd gone to her to get a better scent of her flesh, she'd never backed away. She had really wanted to die.

Clint had performed a three-hour surgery. Not only was her leg badly infected, but there had been small pieces of stone and leaves in it. He'd been impressed with the stitches that someone had put in as well. Connor had a feeling that she'd put them there herself.

"Austin said that she's here because of a court order. Vagrancy, I think he said, or something like it. She was in a dumpster when the cop found her."

Connor nodded. He'd read the report too.

"Do you suppose that she'll go back on the street when her time is up here?" Connor didn't expect an answer and wasn't really surprised that Holly didn't say anything. "When I was on duty for the department I saw all kinds of people who lived off the streets. Not many of them survive. And she's been doing it for a very long time."

The woman on the bed moaned and both he and Holly stood up. He was leaning over her when she opened her eyes and looked up at him. There was no smile of recognition, but she did look terrified. He should have known better than to startle her and when she hit him, he let himself fall back rather than try to grab onto her.

"Christ. What the hell did you hit him for?" Holly looked like she was going to attack Ginger, but Connor stood up quick enough to stop her. "She fucking hit you."

"And I'm a stranger and standing over her when she woke. She had no choice but to defend herself." He glanced at Ginger. "Isn't that right? I frightened you, didn't I?"

It took her four tries to speak. He had been told by Clint that her throat would be sore from the tube down it. When she did Connor wanted to laugh at her, but only just refrained from doing so.

"Where are my pants? My shirt and underwear too?" She sat up only to lie back down. "How do I get out of here?"

"You're not. Not for a little while yet. Hello, Miss Cavanaugh. My name is Doctor Clint Burris. I'm your doctor." Connor looked at his friend and doctor as he walked through the door. "Hey, Connor, how's our patient?"

Before he could answer Ginger threw back her sheet. He wasn't sure what her plan after that was, but she'd frozen at the sight of her leg. He walked over to the side of the bed and picked up the sheet.

"It's going to get better now. There was a great deal of things in it and when you'd sewn it shut, it sealed those things inside. Now that Clint has taken them out, it's only a matter of time before you to get better." He'd spoken softly to her, gently, but he wasn't sure she'd heard. All of her attention was focused on the large bandage on her thigh and the tubes running from it. "They're to help with the drainage. You have—"

"Where are my clothes? I want to leave here now." He could hear the pain in her voice and he wanted more than anything to cradle her into his arms and hold her. But he couldn't, not yet at any rate. "Is there a form I can sign to get out of here?"

"No. Not here. We're a different kind of hospital. There are no AMA, or against medical advice papers for you to get out with. You're going to have to stick it out until you're released." Clint sat on the edge of the bed then stood quickly.

Connor put his hand over his mouth in hopes of no one realizing he had growled. Everyone he could see had heard him and he felt horrible about it.

"Sorry, Connor. I forgot."

"Forgot what? Never mind. I don't care. Please tell me how to get these things out of me and I'll be on my way. There's this guy I work for...I can't remember his...Force, his name is Force. Call him. He'll tell you that I have to be released to go work for him." Holly laughed and Clint cleared his throat. Both of them looked at him. "What?"

"Austin was here earlier. He said you're to get the best of care."

Ginger snorted.

"As for you working for him, I think that's been taken care of too."

"Yeah. Okay, so I go to jail." She looked around. "Or is that where I am now? In jail, I mean."

"No, not in jail." Connor cleared his throat. "Do you know why you were out in the forest last night?"

She didn't say anything, but did look away. He could smell her fear. "There was a wolf there. I remember him..." Ginger looked back at him and her fear was replaced with anger. "I want you to leave now. I have to get dressed."

Connor watched his sister and friend leave the room. He sat in the chair he'd been in for several hours and looked at the beautiful woman glaring at him. Christ, she was his mate. "You're in the clinic on the Force compound. You had a very high fever when you were found and brought here. Clint operated and cleaned the wound. During the procedure, he found—"

"Cop. You're a cop, aren't you?" Connor nodded and, before he could continue, she did. "Thought so. Only a cop or a lawyer would state the facts and not give any sort of inflection in their voice."

"I resent that. I was merely telling you why you can't leave here. There was a good possibility that you could have lost your leg. Maybe even your life."

Her laughter startled him. "You think I give a shit about my leg or my life?" She shifted in the bed and he smelled the blood. "And you of all people should know that. Get out of here. I don't know who you are or what the fuck you're doing here, but I want you to get the fuck out of here."

Connor stood up. He wanted to walk to the bed and pull her onto his lap and beat her ass. But he only stopped short of it when he smelled the blood again. He took two steps to the bed and leaned over her. His mouth was only a few inches from hers and he was tempted to kiss her until they were both breathless.

"My name is Connor Force, brother to Austin Force." He touched his lips to hers briefly and then moved back. "You'll stay here or so help me I'll come back here and get into that bed with you and keep you there."

Her face flushed; he was sure it was anger more than anything. Before she could hit him again, he backed off. He was nearly to the door when she finally found her tongue.

"I had ninety days to stay. If anyone thinks I'm going to add the days on that I'm in here, then they're fucking nuts."

He opened the door and looked back.

"And don't come back here."

Connor left the clinic and walked to the edge of the forest. She was his mate, there was no doubt about it. However, she was not just human, but one with a bit more. He had been informed by Austin that she was a bit different after he told him what he thought she might be to him.

"You should know that she's not just a human, but an empath, a person who can read things or something like that. From all accounts she's been one since birth. And someone is chasing her." Connor looked at the woman on the bed who'd just been brought into her room.

"Do we know who or why?" Connor figured someone would want her for her looks alone, but knew that it was because of her abilities. *"Do you have a rundown on some of the run-in's that she's had?"*

"I have a list that George gave me. It has all her foster homes, as well as addresses. And no, we don't have a clue who, but the why? I'm pretty sure you can figure it out." Austin looked at her.

Jealously flared, but he didn't say anything.

"She's your mate."

Connor nodded. "I figured that out when she was begging me to kill her. She offered me her throat without hesitation. Do you have any idea what that did to me? She wanted...no, she begged me to kill her."

And now he had pissed her off and been thrown out of her room. Connor looked back to the room he knew that she was in. And what the hell was he supposed to do now? She wasn't going to come to him easily and, right now, Connor wasn't sure if he wanted easy or not.

~~~

Lou leaned back against the mattress and closed her eyes. She was still here. Still alive and kicking. Looking back at the sheet that the man had pulled over her, she pulled it back and looked at her leg.

The bandage was about eighteen inches wide and wrapped all the way around her thigh. There were two tubes running out from the bottom and were snaked along the bed to something beneath it. She touched the soft cloth and saw that at some point, her leg had bled. She wondered if it was okay or should she let someone know? Lying back, she decided to wait for someone to come back before she bothered them.

Connor Force. She wondered why he'd kissed her. Rubbing her fingers over her lips, she thought again of the way her body felt when he'd done it. When her door opened, she groaned when she saw who it was.

"Hello. I heard you were awake. I wanted to see if I could do anything for you." Mrs. Force sat in the chair. "You gave us quite a scare when we couldn't find you."

"Go away." The woman only smiled. These people were going to drive her crazy.

"When you're finished here, you'll have to have some extra care so you won't be able to stay at the bunkhouse. There is plenty of room at the house for you. Connor is staying there with us too because his house was burnt to the ground last summer."

She ignored her in favor of the silent television.

"Do you have a preference for whether or not you are near him or on the opposite side if the house?"

The door opened again and this time it was a pretty little nurse. She said she was here to take her blood pressure and temperature. Lou told her that she'd been bleeding.

"Oh. We'll have to check it out to make sure that nothing has pulled loose." She turned to Mrs. Force. "I'm sorry, alpha, you'll need to step out so that we can take the dressing off."

Mrs. Force stood and smiled. "We're far from finished, Ginger. When I get back, I need to explain a few things to you. You'll need to know them in order for things to get moving in the right direction."

"My name is Lou. And the only direction I want to go is one that takes me in the opposite direction of you and your clan."

Mrs. Force smiled and walked to the door. "We're a pack, dear, not a clan. I'll see you in a few minutes." She left the room as two more people walked in. "I'll be right out here if you need me."

As the nurse took off the padding Lou thought about telling them that she didn't need anyone, but doubted it would do any good. By the time the doctor came back in the room she was sweating and trying her best not to hit the nurse.

"I'm sorry you're hurting. I can give you something for pain." She glanced at the doctor when he nodded to the bleeding wound. "I must have missed something. I'm going to have to go back in."

"Fuck, this hurts." She tried not to say anything more, but he touched the area just above the wound. "If you do that again, I'm going to fucking murder you."

When he laughed she nearly did hit him. But there was a warm feeling in her body and she looked over at the nurse who was putting something into her IV. Before she could wrap her mouth around telling him off, he smiled at her.

"I had to distract you." The doctor was blurring out, his voice far away sounding. "You aren't an easy patient, are you? Just breathe, Miss Cavanaugh. It'll be over soon enough."

The next time she woke she was in a room much different than the first one. This one was like a hotel; a television set hung on the wall. A couch was pushed up against another wall and there were several chairs, all of them recliners. One of which had Connor Force in it, and a man she'd never seen before sat in the other one.

Connor looked...well, she thought cute, but didn't think for some reason he'd appreciate that word. Manly came to mind, as did huge. He was big. She wondered if his hair was as soft as it looked and then flushed when she realized where her thoughts were going. She didn't have the time or the energy for a man, much less one she was sentenced to work for. Moving her injured leg, she realized that she had very little pain. Well, nothing like she'd had before, and she took off the sheet.

She knew what he was. She even knew that he was the wolf she'd begged to kill her in the forest. She wasn't as worldly as some, but with her touch she could figure out things that others might not know. And Connor Force was a were.

There was a bandage. But all the tubes were missing. She was grateful for that. When she left, and she *was* leaving, this way would make things easier for her. Wiggling her toes, she realized too that while she hurt, she didn't hurt everywhere. Before, even her hair felt as if it was in pain. She looked up when someone cleared his throat softly.

"Hello. My name is Phil Campbell. I'm a friend of Connor's and the rest of the Force family. Holly is my...wife."

Lou looked over at Connor then back at the other man.

"I was wondering how you were feeling. You gave us all quite a scare."

"Why?" She cleared her throat when he cocked a brow at her. "Why does it matter if I'm healed or not? Why does anyone give a shit?"

"Because of who you are."

She looked over at Connor, who hadn't moved when he spoke.

"When Clint went back in to repair the damage again, he realized that your blood was severely infected. We had to resort to...other means to get you to the point where you are now."

She had already figured that one out and glanced at the man called Phil. "Again, why does anyone give a shit? And if you think to sell me off to some lab because you think you know what I can do then you might want to make sure your insurance is up to date. I won't go easy this time." She snapped her mouth closed when he looked at her oddly. Sitting up in the bed, she started to put her legs over the side of it when Connor was suddenly there. She didn't see him move.

"Where the hell do you think you're going? Get back in that bed this minute. You might be better, but you're still weak."

She shoved him out of the way and put weight on her feet. "Christ," she murmured. Okay, maybe he was right. She was still sore. Too weak to let go of the bed rail at least and she was hurting like a son-of-a-bitch. But his smirk made her try harder to get going.

"You have to be the most stubborn…what the hell are you trying to prove anyway?"

"She's trying to get away from you there, big boy. I would tend to agree with her if I didn't know for a fact that it would do her little to no good. For either of you." They both looked at Phil. "You might as well give it up, girl. The Fates have decided and you and he are in for the long haul."

Ignoring both men, she moved to the bathroom slowly. Connor walked beside her as if it was his job. She didn't know what she was supposed to say to the man, but she didn't want to deal with him right now. After closing the door in Connor's face she picked up the new toothbrush and paste and brushed her teeth twice. After using the toilet, she made her way back to the room to find her clothes.

"He's right, you know."

She glanced at Connor and noticed that the other man was gone.

"You and I have a great deal to talk about and to work out. As for you leaving, I've cleared it with Clint. He said I could watch you just as well from home. So if you really want, I can take you there."

"If by home you mean that bunk house sort of place then I'm ready to go. Anything else and it's no. I have a service to perform and I plan to get it over with as soon as possible. So if you don't mind, get the hell out. I need to get dressed and back to work."

CHAPTER 4

Connor did step out of the room, but he waited in the hall for her. He was still trying to wrap his mind around the fact that she'd known he was a wolf, yet didn't say anything. His phone ringing nearly had him yelp.

"Phil just called. He said your mate is leaving the hospital. Is that true? He also said she gave you a hard time." Before he could answer him, Austin continued on. "She's going to be wonderfully bitchy, isn't she? I'm thrilled more than I can tell you. I hope like hell she fights you to the end until you claim her."

Claim her. "I don't know about that. I think I'm going to give that some time. She doesn't like me very much...well, I don't think she likes anyone."

Austin laughed and Connor flushed. "I would say that that's a fair assessment. But you can handle her. She just needs to have someone love her and she'll come around."

Connor looked up when she came out of her room in a wheel chair. Love her? No, he didn't. He was sure that he would eventually, but not at the moment. He told his brother he had to go and closed his phone and moved toward her. "Come on. I'll take you back to the compound. There are things we have to talk about." He nearly reached for the chair, but stopped when she stiffened. The nurse continued down the hall with them. "No one is going to hurt you, especially me."

"And what is it you want then if you don't want to hurt me? Sex? No thanks. I don't do sex. Ever. Money?" She snorted. "I have none of that either or I wouldn't be here. If you want something you think I'll give you because of what I am then you're shit out of luck there too. I don't perform, nor do I help assholes."

Connor was tempted. More than tempted to show her that she could and would have sex with him. And she'd enjoy it. He rubbed his hand through his hair and looked around to see who was close enough to let him take out his frustrations on. Seeing no one he could beat the living shit out of, he looked back at her. Leaning to her ear, he nearly backed off when she whimpered.

"If I wanted you to, I could have you begging me for a good fuck in no time. As for money? I have more than you could spend in two lifetimes. As for what you can do? As you've put it so eloquently, I could give a shit what you can do." He straightened up and felt like shit when he saw the fear there. "I'm taking you to the compound. After that, we'll talk. About a great many things."

She moved down the hall with him when he took her chair. He wasn't sure what he'd have done if she'd asked him about what they had to talk about. He wished she'd been pissed, fought back. Something. But her fear wasn't want he wanted. And he felt like pond scum for making her feel that way.

The ride back was made in complete silence on her part. He'd asked her about her prescription and she'd not answered. He asked her if she was hungry and again, nothing. Finally, he just gave up, pulled in front of the drug store, and called Clint on his way in. He was careful, however, to take the keys with him.

"Did you give her anything for pain?"

Clint laughed.

"Thanks for letting me take her home with me. I was afraid she'd bolt at the first opportunity." He wasn't just afraid, he was willing to bet his life on it.

"No problem. And yes, I did. I was signing off on it when I heard you were already gone. What did you do, dress her yourself and have Phil rush her out the door?" Laughter made him smile. Connor really liked this man. "Which pharmacy do you want it at and I'll call it in?"

Connor told him where he was and asked to have it rushed. He looked out the front window to see her laying her head back in the truck seat. He figured she was in a great deal of pain. But doubted very much she'd ask for help.

"Is she going to be all right? I mean, what do I need to help her heal?" He flushed. He'd never taken care of anyone but himself before. "Clint, you said she could go home. Am I going to run into problems when I get her there?"

"Yes. I've no doubt, but not from her wounds. She's going to give you a run for your money, I think. I've never seen a woman…hell, Connor, I think she's more stubborn than your alpha person. And CJ is a real bitch when she wants to be."

He nodded and then realized he couldn't see him. "I don't…she isn't going to ask me for anything. I doubt that I'll know when she needs a pill unless I simply give it to her."

Clint was quiet for so long he figured he was calling in the prescription and had simply forgotten to tell him to hold on. Then he heard him talking to someone else. He could hear the quietness of the room and knew that he'd closed the door to his office to talk.

"Look, I know you're her mate and all, but that doesn't mean you should have to deal with the things I'm about to tell you. She's gonna be in pain for some time even with the little blood that Phil gave her. The only reason I released her was because I figured if you two mated sooner then she would be changed and then it would over. But the truth is, somebody is knocking the shit out of her weekly, if not daily."

Connor leaned against the counter and closed his eyes as Clint continued.

"Her left ankle shows a hairline crack that may only be as old as a few weeks. How she's walking is beyond me. Five ribs are broken and two cracked. She'll need to take it easy on those or it could become serious. Her leg? Fuck, Connor, how the hell did she even manage to get around much less lay a whole floor of tile? That wound? It's about two inches deep as well as about nine inches long. The stitches she put in? You can bet she did it without the aid of anything to numb it. Her wrist is sprained, but healing. There are two, maybe as many as three recent concussions and one that probably happened when she *fell* and hurt her leg."

He heard his name called behind him and reached for the small white bag. "You know as well as I do that she didn't fall anywhere. I read her file. Someone is chasing her."

"No shit. And it looks like he's found her a few times too many. She needs to be taught to fight back or, at the very least, to shoot him. That fucker is going to kill her if he keeps this up."

"No, he won't." Connor picked up a few things on his way to the front to pay for the medication. A bottle of water went in first then a candy bar when he read on the bag to take with food. He didn't know anything about her tastes and also threw a few bags of chips, a frozen pizza, and a cola. He paid for everything and hung up with Clint just as he was handed his receipt. The man actually told him good luck.

As he rounded the truck he thought he was going to need it. Her eyes were closed, but he could see tears on her cheeks.

Rattling the door handle to give her a few seconds to know he was getting in he watched her scrub at the stains on her cheeks. Without a word, he handed her the bottle of water, took out one of the pills, and handed it to her.

He expected her to argue. Or at least slap the pill out of his hand. She did neither. When she took it from him with the water he watched her put the pain pill in her mouth and drink nearly half the bottle before closing the cap on it. He didn't speak because he was not sure he could. He knew she was hurting and yelling at her wasn't going to help either of them.

Connor kept looking over at her. As soon as her head fell against his shoulder he twisted in his seat and let her lay across his lap. Careful not to wake her, he called his brother Austin.

"She's asleep. Do you think you can fix up one of the spare bedrooms for her? Something close to where I am?" Austin didn't laugh, for which he was grateful. "Austin, Clint said she's lucky to be able to move and she laid a floor for us."

"Yeah, he called here just after he hung up with you. He told me that she'd be better off with a room with a bathroom close. He thought she'd try to go to work in the morning and wanted to warn me." He heard Austin say something to someone close. "Mom said to tell you that she'd help you get her undressed. She said to tell you that she went to the room we had her in to get her stuff and nothing is there."

"I think all she has is what's in this pack she has. Do you think that's possible? That she'd only have enough clothes and other things to fit in a small backpack?" He looked at the woman lying across his thigh. "She's very beautiful, isn't she?"

He didn't expect an answer and wasn't given one. Connor pulled into the compound ten minutes after hanging up with his brother. He glanced toward where his new house was being built and decided that he'd have to have a construction crew help him now. He had a mate to care for.

Looking down again, he realized he didn't have a clue how to do that.

~~~

Lou moved closer to the heat. She'd never been this warm unless it was full summer and, the last time she'd looked at a calendar, it was nearly Thanksgiving. And the bed was the softest thing she'd ever in all her life ever been in. Moaning softly when she found the warmth again, she nearly screamed when the source of her heat growled low. And then he spoke.

"Just lay still for a little while longer. I don't have to be to work for another hour yet and this is too comfortable for words." Then he pulled her tighter to him. "You are very toasty."

She tried to pull away but he was stronger and bigger. "Let me go. Right fucking now."

Connor did let her go a little, but not enough for her to get away. He looked down at her from his pillow and smiled. "I think you snuggled up to me, not the other way around. As for letting you go? Not yet. I'm just beginning to like this feeling."

His leg moved over hers and she stilled. He didn't do anything more but drape his leg over her thigh and not move any more. Every part of her body was screaming at her to run.

"I've told you before I'm not going to hurt you. I wasn't even going to get into bed with you, but you had a bad dream I guess and I didn't want to leave you again."

She didn't remember her dream, but she'd had bad ones her entire life and didn't doubt his words.

"The baby is just down the hall and I was afraid you'd wake him if you cried out again."

"I'm awake now so you can just go back to wherever you came from." He still hadn't moved and she was afraid to. Sort of had the thought of not dancing in front of a beast.

"You need something for pain?"

She shook her head then nodded. If he had to get up then she'd be free.

"I'll get it. Close your eyes."

When he stood up, she nearly swallowed her tongue. He was bare-assed naked. And hard. Everywhere. She quickly closed her eyes and then threw the blanket over her head for good measure. Christ, he was gorgeous with clothes. Without them, he was simply...yummy.

"Ginger, I can't give you your pill with a blanket over your head."

She didn't want the stupid thing anyway.

"Can you hear me?"

When he tried to pull the blanket free, she squealed. His laughter ran along her skin like a soft feather. She put out her hand and waited for him to put the pill in her palm, but he only laughed harder.

"I'm dressed now. Well, sort of. I have my pants on. Here, come out of there and I'll help you. And you must be starved."

She didn't trust him. "Just put it in my hand and I'll be fine. I need to...do these knock me out?"

"They did yesterday. So I would assume they would again today. Come on, come out from there. I want to see you."

She didn't understand him and pulled the blanket down slowly, making sure he was dressed before she took it off her face completely.

"Much better. Here, take this. Then I'll call my mom and she can get—"

"I don't want it. I have things I have to do today. And lying about in this bed isn't going to get them completed." She looked around for her bag and panicked. "Where is my stuff?"

"In the closet. Mom washed up your things and put them in there. I hope you don't mind, but I had CJ order you some things to wear until we can get you some—"

"I don't want anything from anyone. I don't have the money to pay for the hospital stay and I certainly don't have money for stuff when I have enough right there. I have a job to do and the sooner I can get it completed, the better. I'm also ready to move back to that bunk house place. That was perfectly fine for me and I want to go back there."

He didn't say anything as he went over to the chair and took a shirt off the back of it. He pulled it over his head and sat in the same chair before he spoke. She knew he was pissed, every line of his body said that. And if that didn't clue her in, then his voice would have.

"Do you have any idea what a mate is?"

She didn't answer.

"It's a sort of wife for me and my kind. You're mine."

She snorted at him. "I don't belong to anyone. As for your wife? No, thanks. I have enough problems without taking on a husband or whatever right now."

Connor leaned back in the chair and she looked at the closet. "It's too far for you to get it without my help. I planned it that way, just so you know. I want to talk to you without you going all pissy on me. What kind of empath are you?"

His question startled her. She looked at him with narrow eyes and decided that she'd answer his question, but nothing more. "I can touch objects and give you whatever you need from it. Mostly it's nothing more than a few bits of information, but sometimes I can tell what could happen in the future." Not entirely true, but it was close enough. When he only nodded, she waited for him to tell her what he had plans for her to do for him. Like her foster father had. She'd go to the tracks with him and he'd make her touch the horses. She would know the winner and would tell him so that he'd win and she'd get to eat one meal. Sometimes, it would be weeks before she got so much as a half a slice of bread.

"This person who is chasing you? Do you know what he wants from you? Do you think he knows you're here?"

She looked out the window and didn't speak at first.

"Ginger?"

"I'm not Ginger. Ginger died a long time ago. Lou is all I am. And in answer to your question, he wants what everyone wants. Money, and lots of it." She looked at him then. "He probably knows where I am, yes. He'll pay you for me if that's what you want. All I ask is you give me a chance to get a head start before you sell me off."

She felt his anger again. No amount of extra brain power was needed to see that he was pissed at her. When he stood she braced herself for the blow she knew would come. When he moved toward the doorway she gripped the blanket tight in her fist.

Before he moved out of the door he turned back to her. "I won't sell you for any amount of money, not now, not ever. And I told you before, I don't need money. I have a very good business going and I can support myself as well as you easily." He stepped into the hall as he continued. "If he comes here and tries to hurt you, he's as good as dead. You're mine, Lou. Mine."

The door closed quietly behind him. She sat there stunned for several minutes before what he said sank in. He was going to kill him. Kill Dean Herman to keep him from hurting her. She looked out the window again. She knew just as surely that she was sitting here that there was no way anyone would do that for her.

Shaking her head, she tried to move out of the bed. She was still hurting bad enough that she knew if she tried to get up she'd fall flat on her face, but she had to pee. The pill was still in her hand and without thought as to why she should take it, she laid it on the bedside table and made her way to the bathroom. She was dizzy with pain by the time she made it back, but she'd done it and as far as she was concerned, she was well on her way to recovery.

The sooner she got better and able to walk, the sooner she could get out of here. People like the man who had just told her that she was safe weren't any different than any other person she'd met in her lifetime. He might be wolf, but that didn't make him less of a man. And now that he knew what she was and what she could bring him, he'd soon change his mind. Closing her eyes, she rubbed her face on the pillow beneath her head. Everyone wanted the same thing. And never once did anyone think of her and what her needs were.

CHAPTER 5

Dean walked around the block again. She had to be here somewhere. She couldn't have gotten far with that beating he'd given her just a few days ago. The damned girl owed him. His wife left him because of her.

'Course it had a little to do with the gambling, but that was Ginger's fault too. Had she given him the names of the horses like he told her, he'd have enough money right now to buy his wife back. That didn't mean he really wanted her; nope, he didn't, but he could right quick if he wanted to.

He stepped into the little grocery store and asked if anyone had seen a pretty little red-headed girl. Dean didn't expect that anyone ever would and no one did this time either, but he always put out his feelers, as he liked to call 'em. Someone sometime would see the fucking bitch and tell someone right on down the line until someone remembered him and called him out. Dean smiled and made his way to the dumpster in the back after being told that no one noticed anyone. Sure they didn't.

This was more like the places where she hung out. Trash is what she was and trash is what she used. Fucking idiot could have all she wanted, but she didn't do nothing to get it. Hell, if he had her know-how, he'd have everything and twice of it.

Smiling, he lifted the lid to the dumpster and stepped back when the smell nearly made him sick.

She'd be stupid to eat anything from this one, but he wouldn't put nothing past her. She would only have to give him what he wanted and he'd take care of her fitting her station. Laughing, he thought about her station. Ginger was trash just like the stuff she dug around in.

Dean walked back to the cheap hotel where he was staying. He figured he had about enough to get him through until the end of the week. He was hoping he'd have had her by now, but she was being cagey again. He smiled again when he thought of the last beating he'd given her.

It had been three days ago, just the day before he'd found her again and she'd fallen in the water to get away. Next time, he'd have something to fish her out with, but he'd been so surprised by her move that he'd watched her float down the stream until she was too far away for him to catch.

She'd been coming out of one of them hardware stores and her hands were full. Probably good, he supposed, 'cause she couldn't fight him back as well that way. But he'd seen her go in and was waiting for her when the doors swooshed open. The pop to her jaw knocked all the things out of her hands and nearly had her fall. But she was fast and had gotten back up quickly. The next time he'd hit her, it had been in her ribs. That blow had done some good 'cause he'd seen the look of pain on her face. After that, she couldn't move so good so he'd been able to get in a few more before some jackass had come up and tore him off her. Frowning, he wondered if he went back there if he could find the cocksucker and show him to mind his own business. Nah, he needed to find Ginger and didn't have time to fuck with some idiot right now.

"I'll get his ass later. Maybe when I buy out that company, he'll be the first person I fire." Dean laughed out loud at his own funny. "People will know when I come around."

The hotel room hadn't been cleaned. He supposed it had something to do with him trying to get the broad that had been in yesterday to blow him. He'd told her several times he'd been kidding. People, women especially, couldn't take a fucking joke anymore. The knock at the door made him think that Ginger had come looking for him, but when he looked in the peephole, he saw the manager there again.

"I would ask that you move on. We've talked it over, the missus and I, and we've decided that we don't want your kind here."

Dean snorted at him and the man flushed.

"We might have the lower end of the economy staying here, but that doesn't mean we have to keep people like you here."

"People like me. What is people like me?" The man looked back toward the office and Dean saw the woman, the missus, he presumed. "Oh, I see. You're pussy-whipped. Should have known someone... No problem, buddy. Wouldn't want you to get in dutch with the bitch now, would we?"

"Now see here. You can't talk to me that—"

Dean cut him off with a raise of his hand. "You know as well as I do that you're only down here giving me shit 'cause she's making you. Okay. I'll be gone by the morning." Dean closed to door in the guy's face and sat on the bed. He was simply going to go. He eyed the television and grinned. 'Course he was gonna make sure they remembered him when he left too.

About two hours after the owner left, Dean had everything packed up that he was taking. His stuff was already in the car, but it was the rest he was waiting on. He looked at his pile.

Yeah, this was going to put him down as the worst case kind of stayer.

The blankets he'd folded nice and neat. The spread was ugly, but he was taking it too. The pillows were tied together with the towels he'd not used, as well as the coffee pot and all the toilet paper. He'd put all those things into the laid out shower curtain. The television was going to be a bitch to sneak out—it must have weighed a ton—as well as the two lamps and the alarm clock. He couldn't take the table or chairs, but he had plans for them too. They weren't going to be fit for the trash heap when he walked out the door. Yeah, Dean thought, he was going to make a splash.

It took him three trips to his car. And another one to take care of the furniture. He'd had to leave the television after all. He'd accidentally dropped it when he'd tried to lift it off the stand. How the hell was he supposed to know that the fucker was screwed down? Busting up the furniture had the guy next to him bitching so Dean was glad as hell that he'd waited to do it until the other crap was packed away. He was pulling out of the shit hole when the cops pulled in. Dean was still laughing when he got to the second stop sign. That's when he saw it. Release to Work Program. Hot damn, she'd be there. Damned girl was nothing but a pain in the ass and just this side of the law. He was grinning when he wrote down the information and who to contact. George Taylor, County Judge. And there it was. A fine list of who was helping him out. Dean pulled the sign out of the dirt and tossed it in the back with the rest of his shit. He whistled as he drove down the street in search of another shit hole to live in.

~~~

Nancy had to sit down. That poor girl. That poor, poor girl. She wiped at the tears streaming down her cheeks and blew her nose for the second time since she'd left the bedroom. Nancy looked up when Connor walked into the room.

"What is it?" He dropped to his knees in front of her. "What happened, Mom? Tell me."

"Oh Connor, that girl. She's—"

"Damn it. She can be pissed at me all she wants, but if she makes you cry then I won't have it."

Nancy looked at him, stunned.

"I'll take care of her. Just stay away from her until I get— what the hell?"

She hit him again with her wooden spoon. She hoped this time she'd knock some sense into him. She stood up, glared at him, and thought about hitting him again for good measure.

"Sit."

He moved to the opposite chair and sat rubbing his head.

"Have I... Did I say to you that she was mean to me? Indicate it in any way?"

"No. But she—" She simply pulled out her spoon again. "What did she do? She still has a lot to learn about trusting people."

"So she does." Nancy sat down. "I went up to take her some breakfast. She was...she was crying. When I asked her what was the matter, she told me nothing, just tired. I left her the tray and went back to fixing breakfast for the rest of the household. I might have gotten a little side tracked with little ones." Nancy got up and went to the stove to stir the soup she had simmering there. It was the lightest soup she could think of to give to Lou.

"Mom?" She wiped again at the tears. "Mom, tell me what happened. Whatever it is, I swear to you that I'll talk to her about it."

She turned to look at him. "She hadn't eaten. None of it but a few nibbles on the toast. By the time I'd made it back up there, she was asleep. I took it away and didn't...I brought her some lunch about an hour ago. I decided to visit with her." Nancy didn't mention that the visit hadn't gone well. She'd left the room in tears, but it had nothing to do with the girl. It was entirely to do with what she'd discovered. She sat back down. "How much do you know about her?"

He shook his head.

"I thought so. She's not been eating well. Well, that's an understatement. She told me that she's been consisting on mostly ramen noodles for ten years." She watched as dawning came over his face. Connor looked at the stairs then back at her before he spoke.

"She can't eat. She doesn't...she doesn't have the stomach for it." He leaned back in his chair and scrubbed his hand over his face. "How do I fix that?"

She didn't know what to tell him. "She'll never be able to live through the change if you want her to be a wolf, as weak as she is. And not being able to eat will make her..." Nancy got up to stir the soup again. "I don't want her to die." She continued to stir the pot and think about how to help Connor when the she heard the door close. She turned to see that Connor had left the kitchen and had gone into the yard. By the time she'd gotten to the door to call him back, he was in his truck and peeling out of the driveway.

She was immediately concerned, then pissed. How dare he? As soon as he came back she was going to take the spoon to his bottom. Then his hard head again. By the time she was finishing up the soup and ladling it into a bowl she was in a rare form even for her. The girl in the bed was not going to be put through whatever her son was up to.

Lou was sitting on the side of the bed when she came through the door. Her face was pale and Nancy immediately put down the tray and went to her. She could see right away that the girl was in a great deal of pain.

"Why can't you all just leave me the fuck alone?"

Nancy didn't say anything, knowing that pain could make a person say things they normally wouldn't.

"I want to just be left alone. Can't you make that other guy let me go to the jail? I won't cause this household any more problems."

Jail. Nancy had forgotten that Lou was here because of circumstances that had nothing to do with Connor and being his mate. Nancy looked down at the covered wound and saw the blood stains there. She'd been up again. And hadn't asked for help.

Nancy looked up at her and realized that she had no one to ask for help. Connor had left her here yesterday morning and had only returned for lunch then left again. She tried to think if he had been sleeping here. And she realized that he hadn't. He'd left her here without anything in the way of support.

"What do you think will happen if you go back to jail? Do you think you'll have a bed to sleep in like this one? Do you think you'll have any pain medication if you need it?"

"I've slept on the cold ground for more than ten years, most of the time without a blanket or pillow. Most winters I have little more than a jacket and no boots. Last summer I spent the entire time sleeping in an open field until the farmer scared the shit out of me when he started harvesting the corn out there. Pain medication? I wouldn't know. The one and only time I took it was when Mr. Force gave it to me. And I haven't taken it since." She reached over and handed her the prescription. "You want it? Take it. I didn't ask for it in the first place. Let me go to jail, please?"

Nancy nodded once. She stood up and reached for the phone. If Connor thought he could simply leave her here without a care as to what happened to her then she'd be better off at jail. When George answered the phone, she asked for his help. "She would like to finish her sentence behind bars. I would very much like it if you could send someone to get her, please." George sputtered twice before she continued. "If you're concerned about Austin, let me handle him. I want this girl picked up today. Now if you could manage it."

"I thought she was Connor's mate. The doc said—"

"Connor has made his decision about her." She waited for him to speak and when he didn't, she continued. "You come and get her or I bring her to you. If I have to do that, there are any number of pack going to be pissed at you for making me wait dinner for them."

George laughed. "You have something brewing in that mind of yours, don't you? I just bet that..." He laughed. "I'll come and get her. Something isn't right, but I'm sure that when the shit hits the fan, and we both know that it will, you'll tell me all about it."

Nancy didn't even bother telling him she had no idea what he was talking about. Instead, she hung up a few minutes later and helped Lou get dressed. The girl was sweating by the time Nancy helped her into a pair of old sweat pants and an older sweat shirt. It had taken some doing to find something of Connor's that had his scent on it, but she just managed to get it on her before the police cruiser showed up. Things were about to get fun. Smiling, she went to find CJ to tell her what she'd done.

CHAPTER 6

Connor watched the flatbed driver take the last of the wood off the truck. It was the second delivery this week and he was beginning to see that all his hard work was paying off. The outter walls were beginning to take shape and some of the plumbing had been put into position. It was starting to look like it was under construction rather than just a dream of one.

"You want I should start on the out walls or you want that I get things ready for the electrician for tomorrow?"

Connor looked over at the foreman he'd hired the day before yesterday. Walter Nolan had worked miracles in a short amount of time. He nodded. "I know it's just an inspection to see if we can get it out this way, but I want him to see what I need done. If you leave me a list of things for tonight, I'll work on it."

Connor had been sleeping at the empty shell for two nights. Not so much sleeping really, but napping only to get up and work some more on the house. He was exhausted, but he needed to have the house finished sooner rather than later. Then he'd spend time getting to know his mate.

He'd seen how his brothers were with their mates. Besotted came to mind. They couldn't make a move without checking in with them or making sure they were all right. He wanted that too, but now he had things to get finished. The house for one thing, and he was expanding his business. He couldn't do those things and be all lovey dovey with his mate. Besides, he was pretty sure she was too sore to get to know him anyway.

He looked up when someone cleared his throat. He thought maybe he'd fallen asleep standing up. He looked at Austin.

"You been busy." They both looked at the shell as Austin continued. "How much longer do you think it'll be?"

"Nolan says about two months. Less if the weather holds. If we can get the walls up, he said working inside will be a breeze." He walked alongside Austin when they entered what would be the main doorway. "I've made some adjustments to the original plans. When I started this, I didn't have a mate and figured that I could add on later."

Austin nodded. Connor thought there was something odd about his brother being here, but he was too tired to try and work it out. Besides, Austin would eventually get around to whatever brought him out here this late in the day. Yawning again, they walked toward where the kitchen would be.

"Do you think she can cook? Lou, do you think she knows how to cook?"

Connor shrugged.

"I'm betting she can if given the right motivation. She probably hasn't had a great deal of stove time being on the run like she has been."

Connor nodded. He was simply too tired to do this. "Spill it. I'm exhausted, pissed off, and need to eat. I'd like nothing more than to go on a run and not stop until I'm so far away no one can bother me."

"She's gone." It took Connor's mind a couple of seconds to figure out what he was saying. Then he clarified. "Lou. She wasn't working so I had her taken back to the jail. She left a few hours ago."

"You did what?" He turned to his older brother and felt his beast snarl at him. "You sent my mate back to jail? What the fuck for?"

Austin stretched. He was bigger than Connor and his wolf was master over his. He started to back down, but he had taken his mate. No one touched what was his.

"Does she know what you're doing? Does she know where you are?"

Connor heard him, but wasn't capable of answering. All he could think of was that she was gone.

"Connor, answer me."

"No. I was going to tell her. You had no right." He moved closer only to hear the low growl from him. "You get her now. Bring her back to the house. If you don't want to help me with her then I'll do—"

"Do what? What is it you'll do with her? Bring her here so she can sleep in the cold with you? How will you keep her wound clean? Spit on her?"

Connor lunged. He didn't like what was spewing from Austin's mouth. Not that Austin wasn't right in what he was saying, he just didn't like it. He shifted in mid air and it still wasn't as fast as Austin.

It was over almost as soon as it started. Austin had his wolf down and his powerful jaws clamped tightly around his throat in no time. And every time he moved or tried to throw him off, he would simply bite a little more. His wolf snarled, but Connor knew he had lost. His brother spoke to him through their connection.

"I'll let you up if you behave." Austin sounded like he was reprimanding one of his children. *"I mean it, Connor. I can hold you here all night if you want."*

"She's mine. You had no right." He hated the way he sounded. *"What the fuck were you thinking letting her go?"*

"That you didn't want her." That brought him up short. He told Austin he would behave and he backed off. They both lay there panting for several minutes. *"Do you want her? As far as I can tell, you've never mated with her. She doesn't even have your scent on her. So far as I can tell, the only thing that you've done is carry her to the bed. There is no reason for us to keep her around when she didn't want to be here in the first place if you have decided to abandon her."*

Abandoned her. He supposed that, in a way, he had. He'd known that his mom would make sure she was fed. After this morning, he knew that she'd been making sure of that. He had felt like shit when she'd told him that the girl couldn't eat anything. But he had thought he didn't have time to deal with it right now.

"She's going to have to come back here. I can't...I fucked up."

Austin's wolf nodded then snorted.

"Can you have her brought back here?"

"No. You want her, then you go and get her. But know this. If you don't do something toward making her welcome or at least knowledgeable about us, then I'll send her back and forbid you to have contact with her."

Connor wasn't sure he could do that, but nodded anyway. He looked over the house again and decided that he'd have to have someone else finish it. And quickly. He turned to his brother. *"I have the funds to do this now, but not...do you have some of the names of the companies that finished up the houses this summer? I need to get this completed now instead of fucking around like I've been doing."*

"I think I can help you out there." Austin stretched and so did Connor. *"I was hoping you'd put up more of a fight. I was*

all prepared to kick your ass a few times. Disappointed in you, little brother."

Connor was sure he meant in the fight they'd not had, but he was also disappointed in himself. He'd done his mate a great disservice. He'd left her. Connor knew that his intentions were good, just not sound. When he and Austin took off toward the woods, Connor decided that starting tonight, he'd make sure his mate was taken care of. And taken care of by him.

~~~

Lou walked around the cell again. She wasn't hanging onto the walls as much as she had been and felt pretty proud of herself. Of course she hurt like hell and she did trip up over the pain on occasion, but she was getting stronger. It had taken her longer to heal this time, but she knew that lying around waiting wasn't going to get her to the point where she could run again.

Lying down on the small cot, she covered up with the thin blanket. The one at the Force house had been nicer, warmer, but she hadn't wanted to get used to the luxury. She knew that it was simply a matter of time before she'd be released and then out on her own again. She did feel bad about the woman, Mrs. Force. The woman had cried when she'd left.

Lou remembered her own mother. She had been beautiful. But when she'd looked at her, she never looked anything but disappointed. And embarrassed. Her parents had been ashamed of what she could do. She remembered the last night she'd been their daughter...

"You aren't to let a single person know what a monstrosity you are. You keep your hands in your pockets and your mouth shut. Do you hear me?"

"Yes, ma'am." Lou had been all of four, but had known then that what she could do was something no one else could do. "I won't touch anyone."

"See that you don't." Her mother had jerked her arm hard and glared right in her face. "If I hear one single word about what you know about someone I will put you up for adoption so fast you won't be able to take any of those pretty things in your room with you."

Lou had nodded. As the first guest arrived, Lou found herself a corner and sat on her hands. She didn't even move when she was told dinner was ready and waiting until everyone was in the large dining room.

She knew that her parents only let her eat with them because they wanted to show people how wonderful they were. She'd had the best clothes, the best books, and furniture. They had even made sure when the time was right she was going to the best schools. But even the best of everything couldn't have stopped what had happened.

She had reached for the glass of water when so had the man sitting next to her. He'd wrapped his larger hand around hers and she felt the connection snap into place. It only took seconds for what he'd done, what he'd been doing for a long time, to run through her mind and before she knew it, she was screaming. Then everything blacked out.

When she opened her eyes her mother was slapping her cheeks. Her face was angry red and tears stained her face. Lou had thought in that moment that her mother was worried so she'd reached out to touch her cheek. To assure her that she was fine. But her mother had slapped her hand away and recoiled from her.

"You monster."

Lou lay there, stunned.

"What the hell were you doing? I told you, I explained to you that you were not to touch anyone. Didn't I?" Before Lou could nod, her mother slapped her again. "You are nothing to

me. Had I known before you were born what you were, I'd have aborted you instantly."

Lou had looked at her father, hoping for some help from him and she saw him talking to the police. She knew then that she'd said what the man had been up to. She knew then that there was no help coming from him either.

By the next morning she was in a large house with other children. None of them were like her, but they knew what she could do. Her mother had announced it to the room when Lou had been shown to her cot.

"Stay away from this girl," she'd said in a loud voice. "She'll steal your soul and make you do things that will get you into trouble. She's a monster, one that lays in wait for you to be close to her then she will attack you."

The children hadn't ever come near her. And the others, newer ones that had been brought in, were told the same thing. After that Lou had tried daily to get away until finally she was sent out into the world to live with foster parents. And they were no better than the children.

Then there had been the Hermans. The last people she'd been shipped off to. Mrs. Herman had only wanted her to babysit the other five children in the home, but the mister had wanted her to give him information. The kind that made him money...

Lou looked up when someone opened her cell door.

"I've come to take you home."

She looked away from Connor and the man standing next to him. She wasn't overly thrilled with the judge standing there either.

"Come on. I've paid your fine and you can—"

"I'm fine right here." She was too. "You can get your money back from him if you want, but I'm staying here."

The judge laughed. Both she and Connor glared at him, but he didn't seem to mind. Connor moved out of the older man's way as he moved into her cell.

"Can't let you stay here, girl. You have to go with this man until things are settled. And you'll be better off there than here in this little cold cell." He was speaking low, but she knew that the man behind him could hear. "Nancy pulled some strings with me and I shouldn't have done it, but...well, she can talk a good game when she needs something."

"That other man, Austin, he said that he would break my contract with him and I was free to sit out my sentence here. I'm not leaving." She looked at Connor when he growled. "You have something to say then say it. I'm not leaving."

The judge stood up and walked out. She sat up on the cot when Connor moved into the cell with her. She watched the older man move down the hall and out of sight. She glared at Connor when he towered over her.

"You will mind me. I said that you're coming home with me and you damned well will." She stood up. "Good girl."

Lou was just getting ready to give him a piece of her mind when she suddenly had the urge to lean into his neck. He smelled good, delicious even. When he gripped her arms she thought he was going to push her away from him and was surprised and pleased when he pulled her closer.

"Lick my throat." His voice was low, sexy, and warm. "Lick along the vein and taste me."

She did as he'd commanded and moaned. Christ, he tasted like sex. Before she could pull away, he tangled his fingers into her hair and held her there. She thought he said "bite," but didn't know for sure until he said it again.

Biting him seemed like a wonderful idea. The thought of sinking her teeth into his flesh sounded good, very good as a matter of fact. Licking him again, she nipped at his flesh and was rewarded by a deep rumbling from his mouth, a groan that made her wet to hear it again.

He tore her from his neck and took her mouth. Lou had been kissed before. A quick peck on the mouth from someone she'd known, but nothing like this. When his hand slid down her body and cupped her ass, pulling her tight to him, she threw back her head and moaned loudly.

His cock was hard against her. Moving her feet, she could feel him in her folds, could almost feel him enter her. His growl made her want more from him, everything from him. He lifted her up and moved her back. The wall behind her was hard and cold; the man in front of her was hard and hot.

She wanted to wrap herself around him. Wanted to feel him touch her skin, nip at her flesh, and take her. When she lifted her leg he held her up that way as he rocked into her. She was so close to something that she lifted her other leg without thinking.

He tore from her when she cried out. When she started to fall forward, the pain in her leg so intense, she knocked his hands away when he tried to catch her. He simply lifted her into his arms and took her to the cot.

"I'm sorry. I didn't mean for it to go that far here."

She looked up at him, the pain in her leg forgotten momentarily.

"I meant to take you home first then mate with you so you wouldn't be able to leave me."

"Really?" her voice dripped with sarcasm. There was no way he could have missed it, but apparently he had.

"Yes. If we mate then you will have to stay with me. You'll also not be able to harm me. We'll be a couple."

Lou struggled to get off his lap. As soon as her feet hit the floor, she moved to the other side of the cell. It was that or strangle him. She stiffened when he stood as well. "You say once we're mates or whatever then I won't be able to harm you."

He nodded.

"But for now I can. I wouldn't come any further if I were you."

He stopped and grinned at her. She was sure that had worked on other women, but she, he would soon discover, was not other women. He took one then another step forward.

"Now, Lou honey. You know as well as I do that we can't not let this happen between us. This is much bigger than either of us can—"

As soon as his head hit the floor she stepped over him and out of the cell. *Bigger my ass*, she thought as she went out of the labyrinth of halls in the sub level of the jail. Stopping at the desk, she asked if she was free to go and left. She started to tell the man at the desk about Connor, but thought he'd come around soon enough.

CHAPTER 7

Connor was pissed. He pulled into the compound, tires throwing rock and dust everywhere. He was out of his truck before the engine died completely. His mother was standing on the front porch when he stepped onto the first step.

"You won't go into this house with that much anger." She held her ever present spoon in front of her like a shield. "I won't have you going to her mad like you are."

"She fucking hit me." He flushed when she raised her brow. "She hit me in the head and left me on the floor to…to who knows what. Am I supposed to just let her do that and get by with it? I'm her mate, damn it."

"She told me what you said to her."

He frowned. He'd not said anything bad to her.

"You actually told her that you were going to mate with her to keep her in line? Connor Force, what is wrong with you?"

He hadn't said that. Had he? He tried to think of what he'd said. "I told her that she'd not be able to harm me once we were mated. And that's the truth." The tapping foot made him try to think harder. "I also told her that she'd not be able to leave me."

"And that is the most romantic thing you could say to a woman who spent three days in the hospital then a day in a cell? Mate with me so you have to come to heel."

Connor started to glare at her and thought better of it. That fucking spoon hurt when she caught you between the eyes like she did. He looked up at the second floor to the pack house where he knew she was. "She's not cooperating with me." He sat on the step and put his head in his hands. "She doesn't want anything to do with me either. How am I supposed to protect her when she keeps running away?"

He felt his mom sit next to him and put her arm around him. "I know you read her file. You know what she's been up against. And Austin told you she had trust issues. What do you think you'd do if she told you something for your own good? Like for instance, 'stay here,' or 'do as I say?' You wouldn't like it any better than she does. Would you?"

He shook his head. "But she's hurt. And in a great deal of pain. How am I supposed to just let her go about her way when I know she can barely walk?"

"You just do. She's not your run of the mill girl, Connor. She has abilities more profound than yours. She can't shift, but...can you imagine what she finds out when she touches someone? Can you even begin to think what she gets from anyone when she comes into contact with them? Connor, she knows everything there is to know about all of us even without us telling her."

He looked beyond the yard to the woods. He'd never thought of her knowing his mind. He knew what she could do, or at least what the file said she could do, but not anything more. He glanced at his mom. "She doesn't trust me because I've given her no reason to. I've been bullying her since she came into my life. And me into hers." His mom patted him on the back and stood. "How do you know? How do you know that she's...what?"

"Overwhelmed? Look around you, Connor. There are over a thousand people here. How many of them do you think have touched her in some way? Brushed against her? Touched something she touches? She's been on her own for many years living out of trash cans and dumpsters. How many less people has she come in contact with up until now?"

Connor heard his mom go into the house as he continued to sit on the step. Overwhelmed. He'd been doing that to her as well. Lou had been in constant contact with someone since she'd been found in the woods. Connor stood up. He had to make it right with her. But first, he had something he needed to do.

He got into his truck and went into town. A man with the kind of money he had could make things happen much quicker than one who didn't. And Connor wanted to make things happen. The first stop had been to the construction company that was working on his home. The next few were to get things to overwhelm his pretty mate in a positive way.

Connor arrived back at the compound late. The house wasn't completely dark, but he knew that most of the people inside were in bed. He entered the house through the kitchen and wasn't really surprised to see CJ there. She was working on something and looked up at him when he cleared his throat.

"I was making her a chart. I know she hasn't been introduced to a lot of us yet, but I thought a sort of pecking order might help her out. I know it would have me."

He glanced down at the sheet and nodded. "She could probably use it, but wait before giving it to her. I need to...I want to..." He sat down in the chair and held his packages to his chest. "I'm trying to woo her."

CJ put out her hand and he gave her two of the bags. "This is nice. What made you think to get her this?"

It was one of those reader things. He'd seen her reading when he'd been in the room a couple of times, and when he'd gone to the jail, she had four or five books open and spread on the floor under the bed. He told CJ this.

"She'll love it. It's much easier to carry around than a book sometimes. I have one by the bed. And I have stories on it that I read the twins at night." She handed it back to him as she opened the next bag.

This one had been the hardest to figure out. He'd never bought women's clothes before and he hadn't a clue what size she wore. But when CJ held it up, he could see that it was silly and reached for it.

"I love these, Connor. And she will too. Oh my, but they're so soft." The jammies in her hand looked as much. "You did well with these."

She put them back in the bag, but not before she rubbed them on her cheek again. Connor flushed and handed her the next two bags. The last bag was stuff he'd keep to himself. CJ smiled over the box of dark chocolates and grinned at him over the strawberries and cream.

"Mom said she wasn't eating well. I thought fruit would help her regain her strength." He dropped his head as he put them back in the bag. CJ's laughter was soft and he was embarrassed. "I just want her to get better."

"Of course you do. We all do. She's very hurt." He looked up at her. "I don't just mean her body, but her heart as well. I know just what she feels like to be rejected by a parent and both of hers did it to her. Poor girl." She turned back to him once more. "And Connor? You have to be honest with her. She won't...she deserves nothing less than that."

He nodded as she left the room. CJ had gone through a lot and he had forgotten about that. He moved toward the stairs and thought about how best to approach Lou. He grinned when he thought with armor plating might be best.

~~~

She heard him walking up the stairs. The house creaked a great deal and she wondered if anyone else was aware of it. She turned to him in mid pace when he opened the door behind her. He had his hands full and she started toward him when she noticed that he was smiling at her.

It was the most beautiful thing she'd ever seen. She tried to remember the last time anyone had ever smiled at her when not making fun of her or worse. She took a step back when he shut the door behind him with his foot.

"I got some things for you. Nothing much. I just noticed that my shirts were a little big on you and thought you'd like something softer to wear to bed." He handed her one of the bags. "The lady at the store said that they were warm too."

She took the bag from him and pulled out the bright pink fuzzy pajamas. When she put them close to her cheek, she looked at him. He was busy with another one of the bags and motioned for her to come closer.

"You didn't have to do this. I'm just fine sleeping in the other shirt I own." She moved closer, but not enough where he could touch her. "You should save your money for someone else."

He laughed and handed her a box. "It's a reader thing. There are some books on it. Mostly classics because they came with it for free. But I had the man at the bookstore set you up with an account. You can download...I think he said seventy-five books, on it according to the gift card that came with it. Anything you'd like. Myles has been reading this book by a vampire friend of Phil's. I guess you might like those too."

"Why?" He looked at her with that smile again. She tried her best to ignore it and asked again. "Why are you suddenly being nice to me?"

"I should have been nice to you from the beginning. But I was an ass instead." She nodded and he laughed again. "You could say that I'm turning over a new leaf."

"I don't want you to turn over anything for me. I need to get going on this sentence so I can move on." She put the things on the dresser next to her and ran her fingers over the soft material again before she continued. "I won't do whatever it is you want me to do. I wouldn't do it for him and I won't do it for you."

"Touch me." She took a step back when he advanced toward her. "You can see the future, right? Then touch me and tell me what you see between us. What I can do for you."

She laced her fingers together behind her and took another step back. "No. I won't. You've no idea what it does to...you have no idea what happens to people when I touch them. They feel...the connection is very strong."

"I trust you. Very much." He was close enough that she could feel his heat and when he put his hands on her arms, she shivered from the contact. "Do you just use your hands, or something else, to make contact?"

"My hands. But I won't do it. It's...I'm not a parlor act." He smiled bigger. She wanted to tell him to stop that, but he was leaning into her neck now and licking her throat. "You have to quit that. It's not...it's not fair."

"But you taste delicious to me. I can smell your arousal. Do you know what it does to me?" He nipped at her skin. "Tell me what it makes you feel like when I do this to you."

"Please." Her hands were suddenly in front of her and she was close to touching him. "I know what you are. All of you.

You won't be able to hide anything from me. I'll…" He licked her pounding pulse. "I'll…please stop, I can't think."

He pulled his head up from her shoulder and looked at him. His eyes were the same warm brown that they had been the night she'd begged him to kill her. Without thought as to what she was doing to either of them she touched his face with both hands.

The memories came first. His father dying, his mother crying a great deal. Fights with his brothers, his first change. She found his first love, his first sexual encounter. There were teenage drunken runs through the fields, as well as sex with a she-wolf. His happiness at making his first thousand dollars then his million. He had even made his first five hundred million and no one but him, and now her, knew about it. Then as the memories grew older, he grew older, as well as his family. The boys that had come to live with them, Reid and Randy, and his talk with them about sex and women. She laughed when the older boy embarrassed Connor when he'd asked about masturbation. Then she saw his thoughts of her, of them. The house that he was building with her in mind. The care he was taking to make it special for her. She knew she was coming to the end of the now time when she saw what he'd purchased in the last bag. Then things changed.

He was hurt badly. His fur bloodied and matted with it. His leg broken and hurt. She saw her standing over him, a gun in her hand and a look of determination on her face. Others were behind her and him, pack. Some of them shifted into wolf, others in human form, but all of them ready to stand behind them, behind her. When she felt the final connection, she felt the room spin and darken. She was slipping away just as she heard him say her name.

"I can trust you," she said as she slipped away into the dark void.

Opening her eyes slowly, she was aware of two things immediately. One, she wasn't alone in the big bed, and two, there were two vampires in the room with them. One of them was Phil; the other man she didn't know.

"He's with me," Phil spoke softly. "Myles Kramer, I'd like for you to meet Ginger Cavanaugh. She goes by Lou. Myles is my child and a very good friend of mine."

"What are you doing here?" She sat up only to be pulled back down next to the man in the bed beside her. Every time she tried to get up, he pulled her back to him.

"He's been doing that for two days. Every time you move, he pulls you to him. Annoying, I suppose, but with mates, it's hard not to have your loved ones close." She glared at him and he laughed. "I felt your pain and when I lost the connection to you I came to see what had happened. The power coming off you was...well, slightly terrifying. You're more than people think you are, aren't you?"

She ignored his question and put a pillow under her head to see them better. "What do you mean you felt the loss of connection? I don't have anything..." She looked up at him sharply. "That's right, you gave me your blood."

"Very good. I had to. The second time you went into surgery, you were dying. The infection from your wound had entered your heart and was causing you to have small heart attacks. And Clint was sure that the next one or two was going to kill you." He leaned back in his chair. "I couldn't let that happen. You're Connor's mate and he's my friend."

She looked at the man sleeping beside her. "You said two days. Is that how long he's been out too? I didn't mean to hurt him."

"No, you didn't, but you did give him what he needed. You've no idea what trust can do for someone in his position." She looked over at Myles when he spoke. "I don't trust either very well. Never have. I think that's why I've made such a great cop. But Connor needed you to give you his. And you did."

She flushed at what she'd seen in her touch of him. "He's not going to be happy with me when he wakes. I told him that it would be painful."

"It wasn't painful." She looked down at Connor when he spoke. "It wasn't painful, but draining. Why? Why does if feel as if you drained me like the vamp over there might do?"

She looked at the two men in the chairs as she answered him. "Because I'm not just what you've been told. I also have the ability to change things, heal things so long as it's tiny, as well as a few things I'm not sure they have names for."

"I would say that's a fair assessment." She glared at Phil and he laughed. "You're not stupid so I can only assume no one has trained you. Can you control it at all?"

"I didn't kill him, did I?" She flushed when Connor burst out laughing. "I didn't mean that the way it sounded. I meant that I can pull it in, but sometimes it gets too strong. It's why I don't touch anyone if I don't have to."

"And your foster father? What is it he wants you to touch for him? I'm assuming it's someone he thinks you can control. And I don't know him, but you I do. I can assume that it's something to make him rich."

Phil and Myles left the room as Connor was asking her. She turned away from him and felt him stretch his body along hers.

"Lou? I know it was him. I shared your memories along with you taking mine."

She closed her eyes. "The first time that I knew what a monster was, I was four. My parents liked to show me off. I was there prodigy. Or something akin to it. I could speak several languages by then and was reading at a college level. I don't know how they expected anything less from me. They'd been making me study and read things since birth. The night of the dinner party that was to get me into the best college in the country was the night I saw him."

Connor pulled her to his body closer and held her. Lou closed her eyes, not wanting him to see into her. Nor her into him. She continued with her tale.

"Mr. Dublin was sitting next to me. He had been talking to me all night. Strange things, almost…almost sexual. I didn't understand them as sex education wasn't in my curriculum. I was uncomfortable, but was unable to make my mother understand. No, that's not right, she didn't want to understand. She wanted me to be what she wanted and damn the consequences."

She saw it now. The table laden with food and flowers. Her mother was an expert entertainer. She and the decorator had spent hours on this room alone for this event. She could almost smell the food that had been prepared. Asparagus and hollandaise sauce, rare roast beef, and small potatoes. There were even tiny loaves of bread on each plate with small pats of butter with the letter C embossed on them.

"Lou? What happened that night? What did the man do to you?" She turned in his arms and looked at the ceiling. "Lou?"

"He wrapped his hand around mine. Sounds so innocent, but it wasn't. He wanted me to…touch him, and this was the best he could do without drawing suspicion to himself." She felt Connor's fingers curl around hers and she let him. "The memories were horrific. He'd been raping young children for years and killing them when they served what he supposed was their purpose. He taped them with him. Them and each other. Hundreds of children lost all they had because he was a monster. There was a room off from his, deep into the school where he managed. He called it his gym."

"And he wanted to take you there. That's why he wanted you to come to his school so that you could be a part of his collection." She heard the anger in Connor's voice, but ignored it for now.

"He had taken me there, or at least he did in my dreams. When he touched me, I could see it as if it were real. He had me strapped to a table and he was using things on me that I had no understanding of. But the blood I did. All that blood was pouring from me. And he laughed. He was laughing so hard as he hurt me."

She realized she was crying when Connor brushed the tears away with his thumb. She didn't want to show weakness to him, but he was giving her no choice. She finished her story so that he'd go away and leave her alone.

"The police came to take me away. I had...I guess I had stabbed him with my fork. I don't remember that, but they took me away. While I was being driven away I told them what I had seen, what he had planned for me, and one of the officers turned to look at me. He looked not at me, it seemed, but into me. He had his partner turn back to the school and they went inside."

Connor laid his head on her chest and she wanted more than anything to hold him too. But she didn't, and it wasn't until he spoke that she realized that this man above all others might come to understand her.

"He was like you, wasn't he? The cop, he was an empath just like you, and he knew that what you had seen was real."

"Yes, he was."

CHAPTER 8

Dean watched the house and could see a lot of comings and goings, but nothing that would lead him to believe that Ginger was here. He was about to turn away when he heard someone say the name "Lou." It was a long shot, but he turned back to listen.

"I guess she's forever going to be called that name, isn't she?" The older man laughed. "I suppose it's okay if you like the butch type names. Me? I want a woman who has a name that befits her."

"You mean like 'Bambi,' or better yet 'Bimbo?' For you, I'd probably look for a girl named 'Boobs.' That's all you seem to think about." The older man cuffed the younger one in the head as he continued. "Get yourself back to work afore I kick your ass to the other side of the room. Kids. They've no respect for love."

Dean walked up to the younger man when he wandered off. He was just picking up a large bag of something heavy-looking when he turned and saw him. Dean smiled his best smile at him and put out his hand. "I'm Dean Herman. I've been looking for my stepdaughter for a few weeks now. I hope you can help me." The man hefted the bag up on his shoulder more and didn't answer. "Her name is Ginger Louise.

Cavanaugh, Ginger Louise Cavanaugh. Have you heard of her?"

"Nope." He looked behind him and Dean turned to find the older man there behind him. "He's looking for someone name of Cavanaugh. I told him I ain't never heard of her."

"You a part of this crew that's coming in?"

Dean smiled at the older man; Karl it said on his shirt.

"You don't be looking like you can handle this kinda work. I think it would do you a world of goodness if'n you moved on." Karl took a stance that Dean had seen on bigger men all his life. As if he didn't mean piss to him. He wanted to take a stand, but he couldn't. He was still hurting from the beating he'd given Ginger a week ago.

He backed away and held up his hands in surrender. "I meant no harm. Just looking for a runaway." Dean knew as well as they did that she was here and he meant to find her. "I was just moving along anyway and I'll just be looking elsewhere."

"You do that. And If'n I see you here again, you'll be sitting to piss for a month. If you even could when I finish with you." Karl followed him all the way to the end of the site. When Dean was safely across the street, he bowed at the man and then flipped him off. He had what he wanted now. An address.

Dean went back to his car. Well, it wasn't his, but the one he'd stolen a few days ago. It had expired plates on it and it was hell on gas, but the back seat was big enough that he could sleep in it. And he had the perfect place to keep the sucker. In the parking garage at the closed down mall he'd found.

Dean pulled out his wallet. He had nothing in it as he'd gone to the race tracks three days ago and lost it all. He knew that he was stupid for putting all his money on the horse, but damned if it didn't make him feel good to have a horse named after him in the finals. Dean's Boy had big odds and Dean was going to make it rich. He'd been had.

The horse was as stupid as he'd seen. Didn't even come out of the stall until nearly ten seconds after the other horses on the track. And when he'd been starting to catch up with the tail end, the dumbass horse nearly threw his rider. Dean had torn up his ticket in disgust. He was nearly out of the park when he heard someone say something about the horse being drugged up. That everyone was being given a refund.

Dean waited in line for nearly forty minutes when he got to talk to the clerk. He'd asked for his ticket and Dean told him that he no longer had it. The man simply said, "Next," as if Dean hadn't been standing there. When he'd been shoved out of the way, he'd tried to get back to the counter when a stupid mall-like cop pulled him aside.

"You have your ticket?"

Dean shook his head.

"Then move on. That's the way it's done. See?"

Dean looked up at the sign above the clerk's head and read it. "No refunds without proof of purchase." Dean looked at the security guard. He didn't look like he gave a shit about him or the fucking ticket. Dean moved on. He was out to his car when he realized that the racetrack people planned it that way. They made you so frustrated that you'd tear up your ticket and they didn't have to pay. Dean was convinced that they hung that sign after the race.

"Damn it, why can't a working man catch a fucking break? I just need to make a few dollars so I can get Ginger and take her back home with me." He tried to remember how long it had been since she'd lived with him and his wife and realized it had been a number of years. Ten or so, as a matter of fact. "Don't matter. She owes me. She ate at our table and took up space in our house. She owes me."

Dean found the main address for the company. Force Construction was in the phone book and it was nearby. He decided to wait until tonight to go and see if he could find something on her, and smiled to himself as he walked by one of those open air markets. He would have thought it too cold to have one this time of year, but it was fortuitous for him.

He snatched himself two apples and a bag of carrots. He nearly had himself a bag of oranges when someone yelled at him to stop. He was nearly around the corner when he spied what looked to him like a display of tuna. He normally didn't like canned tuna, but he was hungry and didn't even have ten cents to his name. Running full tilt into the tall tower, he knocked it over and grabbed up as many cans as he could stuff in his pockets.

Eighteen cans, a slightly bruised bag of carrots, and two smashed apples later, he was limping to his car. Not bad, not bad at all. He was set to have dinner when he realized he didn't have a can opener. Dean threw all the cans at the building next to him and went to his car.

"Her fault too. A woman should be preparing a dinner for her man, not hanging out with a bunch of construction workers." Dean got into his car and lay down. "Fucking bitch is gonna make me rich, then maybe I'll kill her ass."

~~~

Conner woke to Lou wrapped around him. He was trying his best to move her away from him when she moaned and snuggled into his neck. His entire body went on red alert. Need for this woman was going to kill him. Trying again, he moaned when she put her leg up over his hip.

He'd held her last night as she'd cried herself to sleep. Connor wanted to get up and go find the bastard that had done that to her, but knew from the rest of her story that Dublin had been killed in jail. Someone had apparently taken exception to his habits at the school. Connor knew that if the man was even within earshot of one of the guards and they knew what he'd done, they would have turned their backs on him. He was sure he'd have done the same thing.

"Lou, honey. I need for you to let me get up. If you don't then I'm afraid we won't be leaving this bed for a very long time." *If ever*, he thought to himself. He rocked into her to show her what he meant and she raised her head to look at him. "I can't lay here with you without wanting you. All of you."

"Why?" Her voice was soft and low. He leaned his head close to her to take her mouth when she licked her lips. "You want me, don't you?"

"More than anything in this world. But I won't be able to stop with just making love to you. I want to mark you, bond with you." He kissed her gently and could feel his hunger grow for her. "Lou, if you don't want me to make love to you then I would suggest that you get away from me now."

She giggled. He'd never even heard her laugh before, he realized, and found the sound of her giggle made him feel good. He wanted to hear it again and again. He nuzzled her neck again. When she moaned he licked the pounding pulse he found there and nipped at it.

"I want to feel you come around me. I want to bite you here when you come." He nipped again and was rewarded with another moan. "Do you have any idea what I want to do to you right now?"

"Yes. I saw it in your mind."

He could feel his wolf snarl at him and run along his skin.

"I can feel that. I can feel when he comes to the surface like that."

He moaned again and rolled her to her back. She let him take her hands and put them above her head. His body was burning for her and he could smell her heat. He nuzzled her breast as he watched her face.

"I want to suckle you here. Take your nipple into my mouth and dance my tongue over the tip." She bowed her back up and he bit her through the t-shirt she had on that belonged to him. "You are driving me crazy with your scent."

"You're so hard. I can feel you all the way inside of me." She rocked up when he pressed down into her folds. "I would like to feel your skin over mine. Touching mine."

He sat up, but didn't leave her. As he watched her breathing hard, he pulled his shirt over his head and looked down at his tented boxers. He could see the stain forming on the front of them. He let a little of his beast go, ran one of his claws down the front of her shirt, and sliced it from her body. Her heaving breast nearly had him howl.

Her panties were soaked. And now that she was exposed to him, he could smell her stronger. Her need made him wild for her. He ran his finger gently up her thighs to the juncture at her legs.

The panties didn't stand a chance. He tore them from her hips and she danced up and down on the mattress while he watched. Her bare breasts seem to call to him, but he wanted to drink from her first.

Scooting back on the bed, he told her to wrap her hands around the posts. "Don't touch me yet. If you do then I won't be able to hold back. I want to sip from you first, take your nectar into me and taste of you."

"Please." He settled between her legs and lifted them up to his shoulders. Connor leaned closer to her and inhaled deeply. She smelled delicious and he was going to gorge himself on her.

Licking along her thigh where her leg met her body, he looked up at her. Sliding his finger into her heat, he moaned when she tightened around him. He knew that she was a virgin and was thrilled that she was his.

Leaning down again, he opened her up with his free hand and took her tiny bud into his mouth. Christ, he was going to die from her taste alone.

"Come for me, baby. Come so I can get my fill of you." Her body exploded when his tongue joined his finger. She not only flooded his mouth, but his hand as well. He drank from her greedily and continued to as she came a second then a third time. Lapping up her cream, all he could think about was how amazing it was going to feel when he was inside of her.

Connor moved his way up her body. Nipping here then laving the tiny red place with his tongue, he tasted her flesh. He rolled his tongue into her belly button. She tasted of things he'd never thought of as erotic. Flowers and sunshine as well as her own special scent that he knew the Fates had made just for him. When he got to her breast, Connor suckled at the hard tips, pulled each one into his mouth to savor and enjoy. By the time he got to her mouth, he was so close to the edge that he knew he'd be hard pressed not to come as soon as he entered her.

He settled between her thighs, holding himself still as he tried to calm his pounding heart. His cock was at her entrance and he rocked gently, knowing that when he did enter her, he was going to hurt her. He kissed her and smiled at her. "I don't want to hurt you." She nodded, and he kissed her again. "You've no idea how happy I am that I'm going to be your first, but I really wish that I could take you as hard as I'd like."

"I'm not naive or anything. I just never...sex was never anything I thought I'd care all that much for." Lou wrapped her feet over his calves. "Connor, do you think maybe you could...I don't know, just do it?"

He laughed. "Yes. I could. And I want to very much. But I also hate hurt—" She rocked up, using his body as leverage. When she moaned again, he moved into her deep, punching through her virginity quickly. He stilled when she cried out.

"Please, just give me a minute."

He didn't move, afraid to, if he was honest with her.

"You're bigger than I thought. Maybe this wasn't such a good idea."

He could hear her fear and her pain. Moving slowly he rocked into her again. When she stiffened, he stopped, but moved again when she rocked up to meet him. This slow movement went on for several minutes until he thought for sure he was going to die from it.

Just when he thought she might be right, Lou wrapped her fingers into his hair and held his face in her hands. She looked deep into his eyes and he was sure into his soul. He let her. Knowing that she had so very little trust, he wanted her to feel good about their new relationship.

"You really don't want to hurt me, do you?"

Connor shook his head.

"I've never meet anyone like you before. You don't really want anything from me other than to be your mate."

"And to me, that's more than I ever hoped to receive from a woman. I knew that you were out there, a mate for me, but I never dreamed that she would be so lovely and as amazing as you are." She flushed. "I want you, Lou. I want to make a life with you."

She rolled him to his back and straddled her legs on either side of him. Not touching her, letting her set the pace again, Connor watched her hands as they explored his body. When she leaned down and took his nipple into her mouth, Connor thought for sure he was going to expire from the pleasure.

"You have to show me how to please you. I know the basics, but not enough to give you as much pleasure as you've given me." He put his hands on her hips and showed her how to ride him. "I want to give you pleasure, not the other way around."

"If you were to give me much more pleasure, Lou, I'd be dead. You have no idea how this feels to me. To be deep inside of you. Watching your face as you enjoy yourself."

She moaned and began to ride him in earnest now. Her breasts beckoned him, begged him, it seemed, and he reached up to cup them. Warm and heavy, her flesh filled his hands. When he tweaked her nipples, rolled them between his thumb and finger, she screamed out his name and stiffened above him. Rolling her over, he took her, buried his cock deep over and over as she continued to grip and tighten around him. When she bared her throat to him, Connor licked along the pounding vein and snapped his teeth into her.

Blood filled his mouth as he came. The connection between them snapped into place and he could feel her every emotion, her every thought. As soon as he licked the wound closed, she came again, this time taking him again. Connor lifted his head and for the first time in his life, he howled during sex.

Spent Connor dropped on top of her. He tried to move, he really did, but he just didn't have the energy. When she giggled, he lifted his head and looked down at her. "Never giggle at a man in bed with you. Especially when he's just given you the best sex of his life." She laughed again.

"The best sex of *his* life? Shouldn't it be the best sex of *my* life?"

He nodded.

"I don't understand."

"It was the best sex of my life. And it will continue to be for the rest of our lives. Every day I'll make it all that much better for you." He kissed her then rolled over until she was spread over him like a blanket. "Of course we might have to practice a bit every day to get it right."

Lou rested her head on her fist. She was looking at him from his chest when he noticed the tear stains. When he wiped them with his thumb, she smiled at him. "I'm all right. In fact, I've never been better."

He pulled her closer. He could feel her concerns and started to tell her things would be all right when she spoke again.

"Now what happens?"

He wasn't sure how to answer that. So he decided to tell her that. "We make our way and figure things out as we go. You'll have to show me how to make you happy without driving you insane and I'll drive you insane trying to make you happy. Deal?"

She laughed again and Connor decided that he'd make it his life's work to hear her laughter daily, if not hourly. He held her until he felt her relax against his body then by degrees, his body did the same. By the time he'd figured out that he needed to get up, he was drifting off to sleep with a smile on his face.

Now he understood his brothers and their need to be with their mates.

CHAPTER 9

The office was closed by the time Dean got there. It was a big fucking building too. And the security cameras as well as the big fucking dogs running around it were enough to have him thinking he should have come back during the day. He was on his third trip around when he saw the man standing across the street.

"You might want to rethink your place to rob. I'm pretty sure that the people who that building…" He pointed to the one behind Dean. "I think they have a real hard-on to keep what's there away from people like you."

Dean looked back at the building then at the man. "And what makes you so sure that I'm was going to rob this place? Don't look to me like they got shit inside." Which was a lie. He could see that they had a lot of state of the art equipment in there. "I might just be—"

The man was suddenly in front of him. Not just like across the street in front, but like he could see his nose hairs close to him. Dean started to take a step back, but the man laughed. Like he knew that he'd scared him a bit. Dean wasn't one for backing down and now was not going to be the exception. He lifted his chin.

"Like I said, you might want to rethink that robbery if you want to live."

Dean looked around, knowing that if the jerk wanted to, Dean would be dead long before anyone came along to see what happened to him.

"And you would be right."

Dean did take the step back then. Then another. As he turned to go, he heard the man laugh, but didn't turn to give him a piece of his mind as he normally would. Instead, he kept running. He was nearly two blocks away when he finally had to stop and take a breath. Looking back the way he'd come, he was sure that the man was right there on the same corner, but the harder he looked, the less he saw. Dean was scared shitless by the time he was back at his car.

"I'll show that cunt to scare her poor old stepdad. The nerve of that bitch." Dean kicked one of the cans of tuna from earlier and then stopped dead in his tracks.

There by the car were the sixteen cans of tuna from earlier. They were stacked up in two neat stacks. He moved closer to them without touching them and noticed that something was on the top of them. He leaned closer as the light was so poor here and nearly screamed out when he spied a can opener. And this one wasn't one from a trash heap. It still had the wrapping around it.

Dean looked up and down the street and then back at the corner. There was no one around him, yet someone had been here. Been here and did all this for him. Dean sat next to the cans and picked up the opener. As he tore off the plastic, he smiled.

"Somebody wants me to get the girl and take her home." Twisting the handle over the first can, he started eating the meat inside almost as soon as the lid was all the way off. "Wants me to win this round with her all right, and I can't help but to do just that."

Dean ate two cans of the meat before he leaned back against the car. Full, he tried to think what about the man had made him terrified. He shuddered when he thought of his mouth. Dean would have sworn on his last breath that there had been fangs there. He got up to piss and then get inside the back seat. Things like that just didn't happen except on television.

He had to get Ginger and get her away from here. Something about this area wasn't what he was used to. Tomorrow, he was going to go to the address he'd found for a Force and see if they had her. 'Course he wasn't sure what the fuck he was going to do with her once he got her. He didn't have any rope to tie her up with and he figured that was the only way he was going to get her somewhere without getting his dick taken off by her.

He was closing his eyes when he thought of the man again. There was something…well, scary about him. Dean rolled to his back and looked out the back window. The lighting was off, that's all. There was no way he had fangs.

~~~

Myles walked away, leaving Connor to sit alone at the table. He'd left him with as much information as he had found, which to Connor's way of thinking, was a great deal more than they had had. Dean Herman was not only nearby, but he'd been to the Force building as well. And someone was helping him.

"I didn't see anyone there with him. And I'm pretty sure if there had been, Herman wasn't aware of him either. But someone is following him." Myles handed him a picture of Herman. "He was walking around the building, I believe, looking for a way in when he saw me."

Connor looked down at the photo again and wondered if the guy had any idea how close to death he was for simply being the one who had hurt his mate. He doubted the guy had a clue. Connor glanced up when his brother walked in with CJ.

"You talked to Myles, I take it?" Connor nodded at Austin's question. "You should know that I've doubled up the patrols around the grounds, as well as beefed up security around the buildings in town. He won't get in if that's what he was intending."

"I think he was looking for something on Lou. At least that's what Myles and I think. Myles said he's living in a car. He's got it parked in the mall lot that we just bought."

Austin sat down and CJ sat on his lap as Connor continued.

"Could be he is as stupid as we think or he's being cagey."

"He's stupid." He smiled when Lou walked in. She'd been asleep when he left her this morning. "At least he's consistent about it. Are you going to turn me over to him now?"

"No," he said loudly then took a deep breath. "No, I'm not, nor will anyone here do it. You're pack now and we take care of what is our own."

She nodded and sat in the chair as far away from him and the others as she could. He had spoken to her last night about her desires to die and they had worked some of them out. The rest she said she had to think about. He still wasn't sure what that might be, but he had a feeling she didn't either.

"I wanted to tell you both how sorry I am for the way..." Lou looked at Austin and CJ before she lowered her head again. "I've had a really hard time of it and I didn't have much in the way of choices when it came to my life. I've never had the opportunity to... I don't trust easily."

Austin snorted and CJ hit him. She glared at him before she spoke to Lou. "I know about not trusting. The way you were living, it's small wonder you didn't hurt yourself sooner.

I know that I thought about it a great deal after my mom passed away."

"I was too cowardly to do anything on my own." The words seemed to spill out before she knew it, Connor thought. "I mean, I was willing, but the mind kept me from actually doing anything. I didn't want to be sold to the labs again."

Connor nodded when Austin looked at him. "Dean sold her once before. He didn't only sell her, but had drugged her up to get her there. It wasn't a nice place."

"He won't get me again. Not as long as I can still breathe. Those people wanted…they thought that they could…" Lou got up and moved to the sink and took a clean glass from the drainer. "They thought they could use me as a breeder. Someone thought they could take my eggs and make more just like me."

"Holy Christ." CJ got up too and started to pull Lou into her arms. But when Lou stiffened, she only rubbed her arms. "No one here will harm you or try to sell you to that place again. I'm sure that Connor told you that, but I'm telling you again. No one, not a single person here, will cause you harm or they have to answer to me."

"And me." Austin pulled CJ back to him. "I swear to you, Lou, that no one will do anything to hurt you. I'm alpha here and they know better than to piss me or my mate off."

Lou snorted and Connor found himself smiling. She was going to be a handful. He looked at his brother when he cleared his throat. Connor was sure he was going to say something to piss Lou off and he decided he was on his own.

"You don't believe me? I got news for you, young lady, when I say something—" She cut him off with a raise of her hand. "What is it?"

It was her stance that made him think she was feeling something. When she looked at the door from the dining room, they all stood up. Connor was nearly standing in front of her when Karl walked in. His face was a bloody mess and he was limping.

"Christ." He started for him when Lou stopped him. "I have to help him, love. Just stand still—" She knocked him back when he reached for Karl again. As he started to rise, he saw it then.

The knife sticking out of his shoulder was embedded deeply. In addition to the knife, there seemed to be a note. Connor watched as Lou moved forward. She spoke softly to them as she reached out to the note with trembling hands.

"If you touch it, I won't be able to tell you anything about it." She looked up when Phil came into the room. "You have to make them stay back."

Phil nodded and stepped in front of him. "You know as well as I do that I can put you to sleep. Don't make me have to do that."

"She's going to get hurt if she tries to take that out of him." Connor nodded to the big Irish wolf. "He's in pain, even I can see that."

"Yes, he is. But if you touch the note first, she won't get the best reading on it. Let her do this." His next words were spoken in his mind. *"You have to let her do this because you trust her. She might get hurt, but you have to trust her to do the right thing."*

Trust. Connor was beginning to hate the word. He nodded once at Phil and asked him something that just occurred to him. "How did you know she was going to need you?"

"My blood. She called for me the second that Karl came in the room. She said you would try to stop her and she needed to help this family. As I'm part of this family, I thought I'd come to her aide."

Connor nodded again. He watched her reach again for the paper and when she touched it, he knew that whatever had put it there wasn't Herman. The stiffness of her body made him also think it was meant for her.

"He's decided to help him. The man who wrote this has decided that it's worth his time to help my foster father out. He feels that Dean will fuck it up, but that he'll be there to pick up the pieces when he's done. Namely me. He thinks that once he gets me away from this family, he'll..." She turned to him. "He is going to stop at nothing to get me from here and thinks that he'll be rich beyond his wildest dreams."

"Over my dead body."

She nodded and stepped back.

"Do you know who it is? Anything about him?"

"He doesn't know you're wolf. He thinks you're simply an occult that takes people's money in exchange for letting them live in squander. He plans to call the FTA to have them come out and raid the place if what Dean has in mind doesn't work."

"Think maybe someone can take this blade out of me? I'm also needing a nice stiff drink." She smiled at Karl then knelt in front of him. "You're a pretty lass, aren't you? I bet once you start to feed well, you're gonna be as pretty as a pup under a little red wagon."

Lou reached up, put her hand around the pommel of the knife, and pulled it free of Karl's shoulder. Connor started to reach for her, but she pressed her hand over the wound and closed her eyes. Within seconds, her hand started to glow and Connor could see the blood begin to stop flowing.

Mother fuck, she was healing him.

Karl didn't move and neither did she. Once she sat back on her heels again, she looked back at him. He could see the pain in her eyes, as well as exhaustion. Whatever she'd done for the man, it had taken a great deal out of her.

"I've never shown this to anyone before." She took the rest of the tumble to the floor so that her ass was now sitting on it. "You may change your mind about selling me off now, but you should know I won't live through it if they take me again. I won't. If you give me to them, it will be my death sentence. I won't go back."

"No one will take you. No one will get to you unless through me." Connor reached down and pulled her into his arms. "I will kill for you. You're mine."

"And mine now." They looked at Karl who handed her the note. "The man who did this to me, you should know that he's got a bit of the black in him. Seen it afore. Black magic is staining his skin like it's his birthright. Never known anyone to come out on the better side of that poison."

"You know who he is?"

Karl shook his head at the question from Austin.

"Then how do we find him?"

Lou closed her eyes and Connor thought she was asleep. He should have known better. She handed him the folded paper and then stood up. She began pacing as he read over the note.

"It says that he wants to meet with us. With all of us, and we're to bring his protégé with us." He looked up at Lou. "He means you, doesn't he?"

"I think so. He doesn't hate me like the others I've seen. He wants to show me what I can do with what he thinks I am." She turned to look at them all before she continued. "He will come for me and won't stop with hurting an old man. He'll kill to get to me. I would suggest that you—"

"You finish with that with anything other than you suggest that we join forces and take him out and I will bend you over my knee and bust that lovely ass of yours." Connor stood and stretched. "You belong to me. Now and forever. There will be no one, not anything, that will take you from me. Understand me?" She nodded, but he could see the doubt in her face. There was no real reason she should trust him and he knew it. It didn't hurt any less, but he did know it. He turned to his brothers. "What do we do now? There has to be something we can do to keep her safe."

Austin nodded and looked at the door. There stood the entire family, including Phil's family. The vampires were smiling.

"We've come to play too. I heard there was going to be some sort of showdown and we want to help." Hope Campbell sat down in one of the big chairs and smiled. "You're very Irish, aren't you, dear? I would bet that you're as fully Irish as they come."

"My parents came to this country before I was born. My father is in thermodynamics physics, and my mother is a chemical engineer. They met on the way here and fell, I suppose, in love. I wasn't anything that they planned." She turned away from Hope, but she pulled her back around to look at her.

"They are the ones that have lost, my dear, not you. Had they not created you, then my new family would not have found you. And now Connor and you will be very happy. You will be too once we take care of this rabble." Hope smiled at him then winked. "Connor, my dear, your house is in need of completion. How much longer to do think to take on it now?"

"I've taken steps to have it completed quickly. And I would like to thank you for helping me out with that." He'd heard she'd sent some of the vampires to work on the house in the middle of the night to help out. "You're an amazing woman."

"That I am. Now, what do we know of this new person who has come into this thing?" Hope patted the empty seat beside her. "Come here, Lou. Let us look the note over and see what the idiot wants."

It was well into the next morning before they went to bed. Connor picked up Lou when she staggered for the third time and was happy when she didn't protest too much. He was putting her into the big bed when she pulled him to her mouth and kissed him. Connor could no more turn her down than he could have stopped breathing. Joining her in the bed, he took her mouth again as he slid beneath the blankets with her.

CHAPTER 10

Lou waited in the kitchen for someone to show up. The sun was just cresting the windows when Nancy came into the kitchen. She didn't say anything, but handed her a large tin and a glass. When she sat down with her at the table, she had poured them both a glass of tea and handed her a plate of cookies from the tin.

"When Connor was small he used to raid this can to see what he could get out of it before his brothers did. He was partial to the oatmeal ones more than anything. You like chocolate chip? Have one."

Lou took the plate offered and set it down. She still couldn't eat much of the sweet stuff, but she did break off a small piece and nibbled on it. "I wanted to ask you something."

Nancy nodded as she ate another cookie.

"It's about Connor."

"I would think you'd know by now that he isn't going to let you go. If you are here to have me talk him out of that notion then I'm afraid I won't be able to help you."

Lou shook her head.

"Then what can I help you with, dear?"

"This man that's coming. Why?"

Nancy cocked her head.

"Why do they all assume that they need to help me? I can just go to him and no one will get hurt. Because you know as well as I do that someone, if not a lot of people, will get hurt when he shows up."

"More than likely. But we will protect you." Nancy got up and opened the refrigerator. "My own mate died some time ago. He was a good man. Not the great men his sons have turned out to be, but he was a good man. Here, put the bacon in the pan for me. I'll get it baked while we talk."

Lou took the ten pounds of bacon from the older woman and began laying it in neat rows on the sheet. She wondered aloud if she was to use it all and Nancy smiled at her and nodded. That was a lot of food.

"Connor gets hurt too." She hadn't meant to say it that way, but it was out before she could stop it. Nancy paused, but didn't stop measuring flour. "I don't know how or when, but he does."

"And you don't? Am I to presume that you've seen this in your dreams?"

Lou nodded.

"And when you have these dreams, do they always come true?"

"Most of the time. I can't really alter them, but sometimes they change." She thought about the man from the school who she'd seen hurt her all those years ago. "If I can alter things, events, by telling someone, then things change. I don't know enough about how he gets hurt to do that."

"Is he dead? In your dreams, is he dead?"

Lou didn't know and told her so.

"Then there is a chance. Have you told Connor what you saw?"

"No. I wasn't sure how to. He wouldn't..." She laid the last slice of bacon on the fifth baking sheet before she could continue with her tale. "I don't think he'd do anything different if he thought it would make me any less safe."

"No, he wouldn't. He is in love with you."

Lou looked up at Nancy, panicky.

"You know that as well as I do. He's not told you, has he?"

"No. Why would he love me? I mean, mating is one thing and I can see that it has worked out for your other sons and daughter, but love me? I don't think you have it right." A part of Lou was happy, but more of her was terrified. "There are things he doesn't know about me."

"I would imagine that there are things about him you don't know either. And that's fine. You have a lifetime to figure those out." Nancy handed her a large bowl and several dozen eggs. "Wolves mate for life. Did you know that?"

She had. She'd read a great many books in her life and wolves were always something that fascinated her. She told Nancy what she knew about wolves as a whole. Nancy listened, but only shook her head after she was finished.

"Yes, that's the wild wolf. Werewolves, what we are, can resemble those wolves, but we're much larger and have a better sense of self being. What I mean is we keep a lot of our human traits with us when we shift." The kitchen was taking on the smells and scent of a restaurant that Lou had stolen into when she'd been nearly starved. "We're logical as well and can speak to each other. Austin can talk to all the wolves as a whole or one when it is necessary. CJ as well. She is their female alpha to Austin."

"I thought they were called bitches. Alpha bitch."

Nancy laughed and Lou flushed. She heard someone clear their throat and turned to look at the woman in question. She had a child on her hip and one walking with her.

"I won't be called bitch so they call me alpha person. I can be one, I just don't want to be called one. Good morning, Lou. Welcome to our pack."

Lou put her hand over the small scar on her throat. It burned a little now and then and she flushed when she thought of what they'd been doing when he'd put it there.

He'd joined her last night and she couldn't seem to get enough of touching him. He laid back and let her touch him, strip him down until he was naked. She'd sat on the side of the bed and looked at him, really looked at him. He was beautiful...

"You can do whatever you want to me, but know this, I will return the favor."

She looked at his face and could see he was serious. She nodded and looked at him again.

"Touch me, Lou. Touch me wherever you want. I'm yours."

She started with his fingers. They were long and tapered. There were scars along the tips and inside of his palms. He told her that he worked with metals at times and sometimes he was a little impatient with what he was doing.

His arms were furred in the same dark fur he was when she'd seen him as a wolf. When she ran her fingers up to his shoulder, she could feel his wolf just below the surface. She wanted to see him.

"Not yet. When you're finished with me, I'll shift for you, but right now I want you to touch me." He shifted his body on the bed and took her hand to his mouth. "Continue and I'll tell you a story."

Her fingers danced along his chest and over his hard nipples as he began to speak. She was only half listening to him, but when he said her name she looked up at him. She tried to remember what he'd been saying.

"I was telling you about the first time I saw you. Pay attention." He smiled. "You were naked for me then too. Your breasts are what brought me to you in the first place. The moon had just appeared from beneath the clouds when I saw them. Bright white in the night light, you were leaning against the tree as if you were an offering for me."

"I was out of my mind in pain." She touched his abs and watched as they moved under her fingers. "I saw them, the others. Their eyes were bright like the stars in the sky. Why didn't you kill me?"

"Because I could already smell what you were to me. I could no more have killed you than myself. Why did you want me to?"

She shrugged and he said her name. "I was hurting and tired. I'd been hunted for so long that I...it seemed the best route to go. I'd been thinking about it for some time. I just wanted to go away forever."

"I hope you still don't feel that way. That you have no more places to go, but with me. I want you in my life forever, Lou, and I do mean forever." She touched his hip bone and watched his cock move. Her mouth watered for a taste of him.

"Can I take you into my mouth?" His low growl made her feel things she'd never felt before. Leaning down, she licked along the thick vein that ran the length of him.

"Lou, baby, that's it." She wanted to take more of him into her. Fitting her mouth over the bulbous head, she suckled on him. He wrapped his fingers in her hair and held her there as he pumped none too gently into her mouth...

Lou flushed when she realized that someone was speaking to her. She glanced over at CJ when she laughed. The woman was smiling at her as if she knew just what she was thinking.

"I know that look. I get it now and again when I think of Austin. The Force men are something else, aren't they?" The door opened from the outside before Lou could answer and a woman with a bunch of kids tumbled in. She smiled at them all before she told the kids to go to the play room.

"We've not meet. My name is Alexis Force. I'm mated to Gordon. And Stacy is on her way over too. We'll make a morning of it."

Lou looked longingly at the door and wondered if she could make it.

"I wouldn't if I were you. We'll only hunt you down and bring you back."

"I don't like people." Lou turned her head away. "I don't do well with crowds. They make me...you all make me nervous." She looked at the door again.

A little girl came into the kitchen with her thumb in her mouth and stared up at her. Lou didn't know what to do and looked to the woman she'd come in with. When the little girl took her hand, Lou stopped breathing.

"You're innocent." The little girl nodded and moved them both to the chair where Lou fell into it. "You're so...trusting, aren't you?"

The thumb popped out and the girl smiled. "My name is Sis. My real name is Abigail, but they call me Sis. Are you going to marry my uncle Connor like my aunt married Gordon?"

Lou nodded. She'd never had a great deal to do with children and the ones that she had had been mean and cruel to her. This child wasn't like anything she'd ever seen before. She started to touch her hair, golden and curly, when she suddenly stopped and looked at Alexis. The woman nodded her permission.

The child had seen so much. And been through more. Before she could say anything, the child put her hand over

Lou's and held her there. When she snuggled up to her and laid her head over her heart, Lou could feel the tears threaten.

"The children at the home had been told never to speak to me. My mother had told them that I was there to steal their souls and to kill them in their sleep." The little girl in her arms looked up at her. "I wouldn't have done that to anyone."

"You won't either. There are monsters in my room sometimes, but Gordon scares them away for me. He's a big wolf and they don't like wolves."

Lou nodded at Sis.

"Sometimes, when I get really scared, my sister Darcy comes to sleep with me. She has a new boyfriend now."

The incorrigibleness in her eyes sparkled. And Lou would bet any amount of money, had she any to bet with, that this kid wasn't as innocent as she wanted the adults to believe she was. When the other child, a little boy, came into the room, he looked at his sister before coming over and sitting on her lap as well.

"I'm Tim. Who are you?"

Lou looked at Alexis again and knew there wasn't going to be any help from her. She was laughing too hard. "I'm Lou. And Tim, I didn't invite you to sit on my lap. What gives you that right?" She didn't mean to sound so hard, but they made her nervous.

He just grinned up at her. "You like us here. I can feel it." He adjusted himself more on her lap. "You could help us out by moving on the chair better. That way we won't fall off."

Lou was sitting back before she realized it. The kid had cheek, she'd give him that. Before she could comment on his manipulating her she could feel Connor coming in the room. Her breath caught when he stepped in the kitchen.

He seemed to have eyes only for her and when he cupped the back of her head and brought his mouth to hers she forgot about everyone else in the room but him. It wasn't until the kids on her lap began to struggle that she remembered them.

"You're squashing us, Uncle Connor. Sheesh, are you going to be kissing her all the time like Gordon does Alexis?" Tim made a gagging noise and got off her lap. "Girls are just yucky. And why anyone would want to go around kissing them is beyond me." He glared at her before he took Sis's hand and headed out of the room. Lou laughed as he was explaining to his sister how this place was getting to be as gross as their house with all the touching and stuff. Lou looked up at Connor when he sat down at the large table.

Breakfast was finished up before the last of the Force men came into the room. It looked as if Austin and the other man, Gordon, had been up for some time and that Dallas was getting things organized for a command center, as he'd called it. As they dug into the enormous amount of food, they began telling each other what they'd found out. Nancy set a plate of toast and jellies in front of her and smiled. Connor handed her a small part of his eggs and some of his bacon as he continued speaking.

"The perimeter is as secure as we can get it. I've asked for help from the neighboring packs, to help us by letting us know if someone comes poking around their area. Also, the extra cameras we had installed are all up and working." Austin reached for another rasher of bacon as he spoke. "There are a great many more pack around too, so I'd like to see if you'd take Lou here around and show her where she can go."

"Lou can figure out where she can go on her own." Lou picked up the egg on her fork and ate it before thinking about what it might do to her belly. "And in case you didn't notice, Lou is sitting right here."

CJ laughed and Nancy told Austin to behave. There was a tense moment or two when she thought about those viscous teeth he had when he was wolf, and she lifted her chin. No one was going to treat her poorly again.

"You might want to walk with someone for a few days yet." He looked around the room. "You don't know the ways of our kind and if you get too close to another male, Connor will kill them."

She looked at Connor, who nodded. "Why? Why on earth would you kill someone because they got too close?"

"Because you belong to me." He shifted on his seat when she raised a brow at him. "What I mean is that you and I belong to each other. If you don't know what I mean, I'll show you." He stood up and pulled CJ into his arms. The low growls around the room startled her and she looked at Austin, who was suddenly standing. Lou stood too. There was something very…mean running along her skin. She wanted to kill the woman in his arms.

"Let him go." The words were out before she could stop them. And when she took a step forward, CJ moved out of his arms. Her entire body felt the move as if a threat had been taken away. Before she could sit back down Austin grabbed her and pulled her into his arms in much the same manner that Connor had CJ.

She'd heard the term "when fur flies" and had never known what it meant. But she had an idea now. Both men looked as if they were going to kill each other and their eyes had changed to match their fury. As soon as she was released, Connor pulled her back to him and licked her throat. Every cell in her body felt it.

"We belong to each other. When another person, human or not, touches what's ours, it brings out the beast in us. And it won't matter if they didn't mean it or not." He pulled her to his body and held her in front of him. "We mark each other so that no other wolf will come near you. Not if he wants to live anyway. A human can't see it, but they can feel it. They will steer clear of you because of something in your scent."

She nodded because she couldn't speak. Her entire body was on fire for this man and she was reasonably sure that everyone in the room knew it. So when he took her hand and led her out of the room she didn't fight him. She went willingly. He picked her up and tossed her over his shoulder as he took the stairs two at a time.

CHAPTER 11

"Strip." Connor needed to mark her again and right now. When she didn't move after they entered the bedroom, he pulled her against him and bit her throat. "Take them off before I tear them from your body."

She took a step back then another before she shook her head at him. When he started forward, he noticed the look in her eyes. Fear. Need as well, but fear was right there. He didn't move again as he took off his shirt.

"I'm not going to hurt you. I need to be inside of you very badly. I need to make you mine after Austin touched you." She shook her head, but he ignored her. "There are going to be times when you'll want to do the same to me. Mark me. But for now, I need to do this."

"He only touched me because of what you did to CJ. You provoked him." He nodded as she continued. "Why would you do that if you knew it was going to piss him off? For sex?"

"No. Yes. Maybe. The thought of making you mine again makes my cock ache. And I do want you. With every breath. With every beat of my heart." She didn't back up this time when he moved toward her. His shirt hit the floor. "Take off your clothes and I'll make it worth your while."

She pulled her shirt over her head and held it in front of her. His wolf wasn't happy with her hiding from him and he growled low. Lou's scent changed in that instant. She wanted him too.

"You don't want to make love to me, you want to assert your manliness all over me again." He grinned and nodded. "That's not terribly nice. If all you wanted was someone to chew on, I could buy you a chew toy."

"I have one. You."

She started to laugh then stopped.

"You're still dressed. I'm assuming you want me to tear your clothes from you. You're going to need that new wardrobe if you keep this up."

"Are you going to bite me again?"

He nodded and touched her skin, then moved the shirt from her tight fingers and tossed it to the floor.

"Will it be like last night?"

"Yes. Only this time, I want you to bite me." She shivered under his touch. "I know you can and I can feel your need to do so. I want to feel you mark me too."

"I don't want to hurt you."

Her voice did all sorts of things to him. He rocked into her as he held her hips.

"I can't bite you like you do me. I don't have the canines to do it."

"You can bite me, though. Just bite hard enough to break the skin. And drink my blood." He found that he wanted that more than he wanted his next breath. "Lick along the pulse like I do you. Then bite me."

Reaching behind her, he slid his hands into her pants and tore them from her. Her moan made him dizzy. He lifted her up and moved back toward the wall as she wrapped her legs around his hips. Her panties were tossed over his shoulder as her back touched the wall.

"Connor. Please, I need to feel you inside of me."

He fisted his cock as he adjusted her over him. As soon as he felt her heat he slammed deep and captured her scream with his mouth. Christ, she was hot.

"Bite me when you come. Bite me hard and take me over the edge with you." He knew she was going to be sore, but he couldn't help taking her like this. Need to claim her was taking over. "Do it, Lou. Mark me."

The touch of her tongue against his heated flesh had him gripping her ass to him. He was pounding into her so hard now that the wall was shaking behind her. When her teeth grazed over his pulse, he grabbed her head and held her to him. When she bit him, he felt his climax shoot from his entire being.

"Mother fuck." She suckled at him and he came again. Reaching for her head, he tilted her so that he could do the same, take her, mark her. When his beast came to the surface, Connor let him go just enough so that he could have his taste too. As soon as she came, Connor bit her deep.

He knew what had happened as soon as he took her blood into him. She wasn't just being marked by him, but changed too. He held her tightly to him as he felt her growing weak. He knew now that if he pulled from her, she might die. Taking her to the bed, still held in his mouth, she let him lay them down.

"Don't move just yet. I'm sorry, but I didn't know that...I'm sorry, baby." She lifted her hand and ran it through his hair. He held her tightly to him as his cock hardened again. *"I need to hold you like this until it's complete. It shouldn't be happening this way."*

"I'm fine." He felt her tears on his cheek and sent her his love. Because at that very moment, he did love her. "Will I be a wolf after this?"

He hoped so and told her that. *"You're really too weak for this to happen right now. I didn't even know it was possible. I thought there had to be a full moon."*

She moaned and he could feel her getting weaker. His heart was telling him to lift from her shoulder and stop it, but his instinct was to finish it. He moved slowly over her body to keep her warm. She moaned and he stilled.

"I feel funny." He didn't doubt that she did. "I want to rest now. I don't know what's happening to me."

The moment her arms dropped from him, he called to his brother. The door slammed open just as he knew the change was complete. He was pulling on his pants after covering her up when CJ and Alexis came into the room as well.

"I didn't mean for this to happen. I don't want her to die. Please tell me how to help her."

CJ went to the bathroom and brought out a wet cloth. Connor wanted to shove her out of the way, but stood by helplessly while they cleaned the blood off her neck.

"Come on, Connor. Sit next to her. She'll need you when she wakes."

He looked up at Alexis when she spoke.

"She's a lot stronger than she looks and I'm pretty sure that she'll be fine."

"Pretty sure? I need her. I can't live…" Connor sat on the bed and held Lou's hand. "I knew the moment I bit her that something was off. Why? Why was I able to change her without the full of the moon?"

"Because she needed it to happen. Who knows for sure?" His mom came into the room and sat on the bed beside her. "She'll be fine, Connor. I know this. This girl is going to make a difference in all our lives and this is only the beginning."

After two hours when she hadn't moved, Connor asked them all to leave them alone. He was encouraged that her breathing hadn't changed much, nor had her heart beat. It was still weak sounding but not any less than it had before. He lay down beside her and held her hand.

"I'm sorry, love. Sorrier than I could ever tell you." He kissed her cold fingers. "I swear when you wake up, I'm going to make this up to you. I don't know how, but I will." He brushed at the tears on his cheeks. "I love you, Lou Force. Please don't die on me."

~~~

William Bond moved closer to the car where the human slept. The man was disgusting, but he had something that William wanted. The girl. He'd seen her in action when the human had brought her into his lab some years ago. He'd been chasing them both since. But now he had a need for her that he'd only just discovered.

The girl was the key to everything. Her eggs that were harvested from her had been helpful to a point, but they'd not gotten enough. And now that the experiments that they'd been performing were just on the verge of coming together, they had no more to work with.

Looking at the cans of tuna, now empty, he wondered if the human had any idea that he'd been chosen to help him on this mission. Smiling, he reached down and picked up the opener he'd bought for him. The man simply was the stupidest that he'd come across in some time. But the girl knew the human and not him.

William had been pissed at the wolf when he'd stabbed him. He'd refused to cooperate with him and William, not really known for his temper, had lost it. By the time he'd realized that the wolf had wandered off, he was too close to civilization to bring him back and finish the job. But there was still time yet. Time to get to the wolf and bring the girl to heel.

The human stirred and William brought shadows around himself. He watched as he moved out of the vehicle and over to a wall to relieve himself. William turned away and moved out of sight. There were some things that were better left unseen. When he walked back to the car, William made himself appear as if he had just come upon him.

"Shit. Who the hell are you?"

William couldn't remember if he should bow or simply put out his hand. He did neither.

"Who are you, I said?"

"You asked actually, but that's not important." The man looked as if he didn't understand and William didn't bother explaining. "I would like to hire you to help me on a project that you have failed at quite a few times."

"Failed? I didn't fail at…what is it you want here? I've staked this place out for myself. You have to find somewhere else to live. I've claimed this one."

William didn't move, but did smile. "So you have her, do you? Where is she? I should like to purchase her from you." He'd nearly said again, but just caught himself. "Your foster daughter, I don't recall her name, where is she?"

"Ginger Louise? What do you want with her? She's not…what do you want with her? If you mean to take her from me then you'll have—"

"Did I not say that I would purchase her from you? I am not a man who would steal." Which wasn't entirely true. He'd steal the pennies off a dead man's eyes if he needed the coin. "I would purchase her from you for a great deal of money." William could see the shine in the man's eyes. He was hooked, and for far less than he was willing to offer in the first place. When the man leaned against his home, William sat on a chair that he'd manufactured for himself.

"You have a lot of money? 'Cause she won't come cheap. I have plans for her myself. She and I have a deal of sorts. I let her live in my home and she wouldn't…" The man seemed to catch himself, but William knew the story. "What use is she to you? You look like you got enough money. What can she do for you that I can't be a part of?"

Because you aren't a female with eggs to use, he wanted to say to the idiot. William reached into his pocket and pulled it out. The man would see whatever he wanted to see in his hand and William waited for him to tell him what that was. The man reached forward, but didn't touch. Good, he could be taught.

Long ago, the human had reached for the empty palm and had come up empty handed, as well as missing two fingers. William liked his tricks, but he didn't want anyone to know them either. He moved his empty hand and watched the human stare.

"That's a great deal of money you got yourself there. What if I just killed you for it and took it?"

William said nothing.

"I don't know if ten thousand dollars will be enough for her. I can win that on one horse."

William moved his hand again and waited. He didn't have long. The man did stand up straighter and licked his lips.

"Is there enough there now? Do you think that this will be enough for you to bring her to me unharmed?" William wanted her to himself, but needed the human to get near her. "If you bring her to me unharmed then I will double what I have here for you."

"I can do that. Yeah, I can do that for you and more." The human took a step forward then another. "She won't come easy. She'll…she might get hurt if'n I have to subdue her. She don't fight fair, not even for a girl."

William was well aware of her fighting back. He had a few scars from her as well. Glancing at his other hand, the one she'd ruined, he thought of what he had planned for her when he had gotten all he could from her.

"Do your best. I would like her to be unharmed, but as you have said, she does not fight fairly." William put his hand back into his pocket and stood. "You will bring her to me in three days time. I will meet you here. If you have her, all the riches I wish to bestow upon you will be yours."

The human nodded. As William began to pull the shadows around him again he heard the man speak. It made no sense to him so William didn't bother to go back and see. He was well on his way to having her back. And this time, she would stay put. Smiling, William gave a flick of his wrist and gave the human behind him a bit of his magic. Not enough for anyone to know about it, but enough that the human would be able to take the girl from one smallish wolf pack.

William was back to his home within minutes of leaving the human male. He looked down at his laboratories and smiled again. This time, no one would suspect that he was experimenting, and no one would ever find this place. He closed the connection between the world that humans lived in and the one he was creating.

Soon, he'd be able to move between the worlds with his family. And what a family it would be. Her eggs would produce such a race that he'd be the greatest being in either world. William moved to his throne, the one he'd stolen from the museum so many years ago. He would be king someday soon and when he was, there would be no one to gainsay him.

Closing his eyes, he thought about the girl when she'd been first brought to him. She'd been a mere teenager, or as close to one as she could be. William had already had a plan in place. A plan to make him the strongest mage in the world. But she had something he didn't.

As soon as the humans, a male and female back then, had brought the girl, Ginger Louise, to him, he knew that she was going to help him in his cause. After paying the couple and sending them on their way, he'd had her put into a holding cell to watch.

She'd been drugged, he realized, after she'd gotten away. That was why he'd been so lenient with her. He'd never bothered to tie her up because he'd never realized that she was so strong. But after taking the first harvest, she'd lay docile for so long that he'd went to her to comfort her. And in doing so, she'd nearly taken off his hand with her vicious teeth.

He'd slapped her away and in doing so, he'd tossed her to the door. As he turned his back to wrap his hand, she had slipped out of the room and into his home. He still to this day did not know how she'd gotten out so quickly. He had killed everyone in the household, knowing that one of them had aided her. But no one confessed; no one knew how she had managed it either.

"But I will find out. And when I do she will rue the day that she got away from me." He sat up straighter in his chair and looked over the ruination of his hand. "This, too, she will pay for."

CHAPTER 12

Lou opened her eyes slowly. She hurt and tried to remember what she'd done now, but all she could come up with was a headache for her troubles. When she rolled to her side she bumped up against something and it took her a few seconds to realize it was Connor. He was snoring very loudly.

Sliding from the bed she moved toward the door. Grabbing anything she could put her hands on, she dressed as she moved. By the time she got across the room, she was fully clothed in a mixture of his and her clothing. Opening the door as quietly as she could, she slipped out of the room and into what could only be described as…bedlam?

There were what appeared to be seven hundred children. All of them bent on running her down. When she tried to dodge one, three more took his place. She pressed herself against the wall and tried to think how to get out of this mess when she heard a shrill whistle.

The young girl standing there still had her fingers in her mouth while glaring at the group of short people at the same time. When she ordered everyone to sit, Lou looked around to find herself a chair or seat of her own. But the girl was only talking to the rug rats.

"You've messed up the living room again. The next time I have to straighten it up, I'm going to boil someone in oil." The children now sitting on the floor swallowed hard. "Now, Tim, you and Jake go to the living room and help Sis clean it up. Austin, you and your sister go to the kitchen and clean up the milk and cookie mess you made in there."

"But we didn't get our—"

The girl simply pointed in what Lou assumed was the kitchen. The little boy, Austin she'd called him, bowed his head, but the little girl looked ready to take her on. As they moved past her Lou could see the glint in the girl's eye and knew that once the older one's back was turned, all hell was going to break loose. Lou didn't know whether she wanted to be around or not. She didn't doubt there would be bloodshed.

The girl smiled at Lou. "I'm sorry. I'm babysitting while Alexis finishes an order that must get to the store and CJ and Holly are working on something for Austin. The alpha Austin, not the boy."

Lou nodded, not really understanding what was going on.

"I'm Darcy, by the way. You must be Connor's mate. Tim said you were beautiful."

"Tim. I met him and the little one, Sis. They were..." Lou tried to remember what had happened and realized she was starved. "Do you think I could get some lunch or something? I feel like I've not eaten in a week."

Lou followed the girl to the kitchen and just caught herself from throwing the girl out of the way so she could get to the counter. There were loaves of fresh bread as well as a ham and some sort of fowl. She wanted it all and wanted it right now. She nearly did snarl when someone gripped her arms from behind.

"Careful. You need to calm your heart down. You're scaring the younger ones."

She looked at the children who had been assigned to clean this room. They were cowering under the table and staring at her.

"Calm yourself down and I'll feed you."

She turned to look at Connor and wanted to bury her face in his neck. He seemed to know what she needed and pulled her head to him. His gentle, "just breathe" made her feel much better, but she was still hungry.

Nancy came in from another doorway and ushered the children out. Connor guided her to the chair, sat her down, got her a large glass of tea, and set it in front of her. She drained it in one drink.

Nancy set a large sandwich in front of her and before she could think about it she was wolfing it down as if she hadn't eaten in a month. When the second sandwich was put before her Lou could hardly believe she was still hungry. By the third sandwich, she was feeling much better. That's when she realized what she'd done. "I ate that."

Connor nodded and smiled.

"I don't eat that way. Ever. But if you were to put another one in front of me, I think I could eat it."

"Your body has burned up a great deal of energy. And it needed the extra fuel." Connor took her hand and kissed it. "What is the last thing you remember before waking up just now?"

She rubbed her forehead and tried to think. "We were making love and you bit me. Then you…something happened. I don't know what it was, but something happened."

"You and I shouldn't have been able to do what we did without the pull of the moon. When I bit you, it started the change in you to convert you to wolf." He looked up when Austin walked in. "Austin has been trying to find anything on why it happened the way that it did."

"Wolf." She looked at Austin and he nodded. "I don't know what you mean. What do you mean changed? And the pull of the moon? What does that have to do with me being so hungry?"

"You've been starving the wolf in you for a long time. When Connor bit you, he left his essences inside of you and changed you. We think that somewhere way back in your lineage, there might have been a wolf. And she was lying dormant until someone bit you. Your mate. Connor."

She tried to wrap her mind around what he was saying. She was a wolf? No, that couldn't be right. There had to be something else. Anything else. She rubbed her forehead again. Something wasn't right.

"You had her in you all the time and it took your mate to bring her forth." Nancy looked so sincere that Lou found she wanted to believe her. "You knew she was there. Whenever you needed her, she'd come to you. Remember?"

"When I was in the home I used to think that there was someone watching over me. Not my mother but someone else."

Nancy nodded.

"Then when that man tried to hurt me again, I remember—" Lou stood up. The man. The man at the lab. She closed her eyes and could see him as clearly as if he was standing next to her, but he was shadowed deep within the darkness. She waited, knowing that he would turn and when he did, she'd see him for what he was. "There's a mountain. It's nearby here. Deep within it there is a cave. He has it set up like a laboratory. His play room, he calls it. There are others there, most of them don't even know what they're doing, but know that once he is finished with them he will kill them like the others." She heard someone ask her where the cave was, but she didn't know how to answer them. "He's working on a way to eradicate humans. All of them. He thinks that once they are all gone, once they are no longer walking the earth, that he and his kind will be able to run it as it should be. Magic will rule the world."

"Tell me what he looks like."

She turned toward the voice knowing it was Connor.

"Tell me, love, what does he look like."

"Tall. His hair is white and long. Stringy. He is slumped over like he has a great weight on his shoulders. He wears a robe, though it looks like it has seen better days. His back is to me, but I think if I wait long enough, he'll—"

"Open your eyes. Now. Open your eyes, but don't look at him." The voice wasn't any she'd heard before, but she knew she must obey. But he turned toward her just then and she did open her eyes.

"No. No. That can't be right. No. That can't be." She looked at the newcomer and knew that she knew too. "You knew. You knew who he was."

She nodded then sat down. "I heard that he was back. I thought it was just a rumor, but when Phil told me that you'd been converted without the moon I had to come to see if it was true. But I didn't know your connection to him until you said he was slumped. I didn't know he was coming for you."

"Mom, perhaps you could let the rest of us in on what the fuck you're talking about. You're scaring the others, and I for one don't want a bunch of angry wolves going for my blood right now." Phil handed her a glass of water and told her to drink. "Lou, I'd like you to meet my mother, Hope Campbell. Mom, this is Lou Force, Connor's mate."

"You're really her. The one he's been talking about for centuries." Hope stood up and reached for her cheek and Lou backed away. "I won't harm you. I'm sorry, I should explain."

"That would be nice," Austin snarled. "Maybe you could let the rest of us in on this little story you seem to have."

"Don't be sarcastic, young man. I'm still your elder." Hope sat down and so did Lou. She could feel Connor nearby, but not within touching distance. She found she suddenly needed that. When she reached for him, he took a step back. Everything in her froze.

It wasn't until Phil touched her shoulder that she looked at him. She had a feeling he knew what had happened and wasn't any happier about it than she was. She looked away from both men and focused on Hope and CJ.

"He's my father. The man who...I guess married my mother. He looked different, but...older, I guess." She looked down at the glass of water Phil had given her and wondered about that. "Water. You keep giving me water. Why?"

"It will help you in the healing process. Once you shift, you're going to be fine." He took out a book and handed it to her. She could hardly see if for the tears welling in her eyes.

"Look at the men in this picture. Tell me which ones you know or have seen."

Lou looked at the picture for several seconds before she saw it. She wiped at the tears and focused on it.

"There are nine men in this picture, Lou, which ones have you seen before?"

She pointed to the first man she saw and told him that his name was Mr. Dublin. She didn't know his first name, but he was dead. Picking up the picture, she noticed two more. "That man was the first foster father I had. I don't remember what happened to him, but soon after I left him and his wife's care, he was killed." She looked at the man standing next to him. "This man was the third foster father. His wife murdered him one night and that's how I was taken from that home."

"Who are they? This is a group of men, who are they?" Lou ignored Connor to study the picture more closely. The man in the middle was her father.

"That's him. That's the man who claimed to be my father. I never knew him to be...well, so old, I guess. And the humpback thing, he told me once it was because he was carrying the weight of the devil on his back." She looked up at Hope. "He wasn't really my father, was he?"

"No. I think you're the child of them all. They each had something to give to you and the woman who carried you to term died right after your birth." Hope pulled the book to her as she continued. "There were five women who were held for breeding purposes and just the one, Eva, carried to term. The other men are also dead with the exception of the one you knew as your father and this man."

Hope pointed to the man on the end, the man she knew to be dead. He had been killed in the jail, she'd been told, because she'd told the officer who he was. Then she saw something else. The man in the front. It was the cop.

"He knew. He knew what I was when he came to get me."

Hope nodded sadly.

"When I felt what Dublin had done, my father called them in. They were to take me somewhere, probably to him anyway, when I told them what I'd seen."

"We can only assume that's what happened. We, the vampire council, knew about you, but by then there was little we could do to save you. Once they got you into the foster care system they changed everything about your birth, including your name. And every time you'd surface one of the elders would be killed and someone else would whisk you away."

"But Dublin isn't dead. How do you know this?" She looked at the picture again and remembered the tools he'd been using on her that day. "He's the person conducting the experiments. The one…he was the man in the lab the day they took me in, when Herman sold me." Lou looked at the picture again before she stood up. She walked to the door and opened it. She was surprised that no one tried to stop her, but CJ did follow her outside.

"He's overwhelmed."

Lou laughed at CJ's statement.

"I know I am, and I'm sure you are as well. Give him time."

Lou nodded. "I'm a wolf now, aren't I? I'm like the rest of you, a wolf. Can I shift or whatever now?"

"Yes. You can shift. Though I wouldn't recommend it without someone there with you. It's sort of scary at first."

Lou felt her skim along her skin; her wolf wanted out. She nodded toward the house and then looked at CJ. The woman looked like she wanted to say more. "I'm leaving. I know that there are things that need to be…I don't know what's going to happen here, but I'm leaving." She felt the wolf snarl at her, but didn't let her control her just yet. "You…I want you to leave me alone. Can you do that?"

"I can, but I don't know about Connor."

Lou looked back at the house.

"He's in love with you, Lou."

"He's not my problem. And if he did love me then he…" She shook her head. "Never mind. I'll see you around."

The shift came over her quickly and without the pain she expected. Her body felt long, sleek, and muscled. She looked back at CJ and watched her take a shaky breath. Lou had a moment to wonder what color she was or if she was as big as the wolves she'd seen in the woods that first night. Leaping toward the woods, she heard someone call her name, but she didn't stop. She had to get away from them all.

~~~

Connor buried his nose in the earth again, trying in vain to catch her scent. She was simply gone. He'd been looking for over three hours and all he'd been able to scent was the clothes she'd left behind. Reaching for her through their connection again, all he got was static and he howled at the dark sky.

"She'll come home once she cools off."

Connor glared at his brother, not giving two shits if he was his alpha.

"I would just let her go until she returns."

"Go back then. I'm sure your precious mate can tell you all about the conversation she had with my mate after she let her go off on her own." Connor knew he should have kept his mouth shut, but he was pissed. *"I'm sure that it'll make nice table talk about how Connor Force drove his mate away."*

"Shut up, Connor, before I forget—"

Connor lunged for Dallas. He was spoiling for a fight and he didn't care who gave it to him. But Connor wasn't thinking straight or he would have seen that no matter what he did, which brother he attacked, the others would be there to save their asses. He was down on the ground before he could connect with Dallas' throat.

"He'll let you up when you can be reasonable. You did drive her away. What the fuck did you expect her to do when you practically ran in the opposite direction when she held out her hand for you?"

Connor snarled again, at Gordon this time.

"You're a fool if you think she'll come running back to you now."

"She's not what I expected." That was an understatement if there ever was one. *"I was supposed to protect her. Take her into my keeping and help her with her wolf. She's a better wolf than me."*

"So because you feel she didn't need you, you figured you'd just walk away? You moron. What the fuck do you think she was thinking when her entire life was a lie? We all saw her reach for you and what the fuck did you do?" Gordon nipped at his belly. *"You fucking turned your back on her."*

He had to. He'd been so…so what he didn't know, but she had reached for him and he didn't know what to do. She was more than just his mate; she was a wolf in waiting. One that everyone knew about but him. He looked up at his brother and asked to be let go.

"Will you behave yourself? So help me, Connor, I'll take you to the cells and leave you there." Connor assured Austin he'd behave and was let go.

"Go away. All of you, just go away." He shifted and stood up, reaching for his pack that had been torn from his waist. "I just need to be alone for a while."

Austin shifted as well and pulled on his pants. He nodded to the others, who left as wolves. Connor waited for the lecture he was sure was coming when Austin sat beside him.

"She needs you."

Connor snorted at his brother.

"She does. CJ said she was hurt, but she could see that she was terrified. You have to find her."

And say what to her? he thought. Connor only nodded and didn't look at his brother when he stood up again. The moment he was gone Connor leaned back against the tree and let go. The tears streamed down his face and burned his eyes. He'd lost the only woman he would ever love.

Connor started toward the house again when he remembered what she'd said. A mountain. A cave deep into a mountain. One he knew just where it was. But he also remembered what Gordon had said about the abandoned mall and the man he'd seen coming and going from there.

CHAPTER 13

She knew just where to go. She'd seen it in such great detail that she would have been able to draw them a map if they wanted her to. But she had to make a stop first. She also knew where Herman was.

By the time she got to the mall she was terrified of everything. Cars were loud and fast and the lights hurt her eyes. She tried to walk on the roads, but it hurt her feet, paws, she supposed. But she knew now what she looked like.

It had been by chance that she walked by the storefront when no one was coming. Cars had not been this way in a long time and, if asked, she would have thought that all the displays in the now defunct mall would have been destroyed or stolen, but there was a large window out front that was whole and she could see herself in it.

She was a red wolf. Her fur was as fiery red as her hair had been. Bright in the light of the moon, she looked as if she glowed. But her eyes were what set her apart from any of the other wolves she'd seen at the house. Hers were the color of emeralds.

Dark green, they didn't reflect back like Connor's had, or any of the other wolves'. Hers were dark enough that she could see out, but was sure that no one would be able to see her. She had never even heard of a green-eyed wolf. Lou knew that she would be considered a very handsome wolf.

Grinning, she walked up to the highest level in the garage and found his scent. She didn't even realize that was what she'd been following until she could see him. And he was talking to himself. Or so she thought.

"I don't know how much money he was talking about, but it was a lot." He was eating something out of a can and Lou thought it was tuna. "Yes, sir, lots of it too. As soon as you give her over to me then we'll both be rich."

"Yeah, so you said."

She nearly whimpered when she heard Connor's voice.

"Tell me what you know about her. There has to be a reason that this man wants her so badly. Badly enough to pay you a great deal of money."

"Didn't say. Didn't say. But you'll be rich too."

Lou looked around the wall she was hiding behind and looked right into Connor's face. He didn't move, but nodded at her.

"You listening to me?"

"Yes. I'm listening to you now. I should have listened to you all along, but I was a fool." She had a feeling he wasn't talking to Dean any longer. "You and I should have partnered from the beginning and none of this would have been necessary."

"Partnered? Hell, boy, I didn't even know you 'til you showed up practically at my doorstep. Want some tuna? Don't care much for it myself, but it's sticking to the bones. Yeppers, it does."

She reached for his mind. Something she'd only just figured out she could do. *"He means to kill you. Herman there. He means to kill you."*

Connor looked back at the man on the ground. *"He might mean to, but with you by my side I'm pretty sure we can whip his ass."*

Lou took a deep breath and moved out into the opening. She watched Connor to see what his move would be. When he bowed before her, she nodded her head. That was when Herman saw her. She turned to look at him and snarled with a low growl from her throat.

"Holy Christ. It's a big fucking dog." He stood up and tried to get behind Connor. "Kill that sucker before he eats us. He probably has rabies or something. Kill it."

"I don't think so." She walked closer to Connor and sat beside him. When he reached out and rubbed her behind her ear, she leaned into him. "This is my mate. And right now, you're going to be her dinner if you don't tell us where the man who hired you is."

"Mate? What the fuck...are you one of those sick boys who does it with animals? Holy mother of fucktards. You are one sick shit." Herman backed from them both as he pulled out a gun and aimed it at Connor. Her Connor. "Get away from here and take the dog with you."

Lou lunged. When she did, she felt the animal in her respond. As soon as she was airborne she felt her take over and the need to protect Connor kick in. Before she took him to the ground she knew he was dead. The blood that filled her mouth gave her a sense of power, a power so great she threw back her head and howled.

When she felt a ripple in the air she turned to Connor coming toward her. He was magnificent. He was huge and he was hers. Moving off the dead body, she moved toward him. The ripple in her skin made her aware of what was happening. She was becoming a human again.

Connor caught her when she leapt toward him. His body cushioned her as they went to the ground. Even before she was completely shifted he was stripping his own clothes off and touching her, tasting her.

"I need you. I need to fill you with my cock right now."

She moaned as he bit at her breast. Her body was not just ready for him, but hot lava seemed to run through her veins; need for him took her breath away and she could feel her heart pound in urgency for him.

"Please. You have to mark me again. I need to feel you now." He growled again. "Connor, please hurry."

As he rolled her to her back, he slammed into her. His cock didn't just fill her, but seemed to become a part of her, a vital part. As she wrapped her legs around his hips, he took her over the edge not once, not twice, but three times. Claws bit into her back as she held him deep. The harder he took her, the more she wanted. When his teeth sank into her neck, she screamed. Not in pain, but in pleasure. Her body soared up and over the edge a final time when she leaned up and took his throat as well.

Connor came then. Blood filled her mouth as his cock filled her body. And she knew. Knew in that moment that she had conceived. A child was made. Their child.

As she felt the room surrounding them darken, she smiled. They were mated now and nothing on this earth would come between them. Connor growled again when she lifted her hand to his face. "I love you. I think I have for my entire life."

He kissed her gently as she closed her eyes. "And I love you."

~~~

William felt the death. He knew the exact moment that the human had died. Closing his eyes he tried to see his death, but darkness prevailed and all he could see was red blood and red fur. Screaming out his frustration, he killed four of his lab workers and injured another half dozen. Fucking wolves.

William hated canines. More than anything, he hated the smelly doglike creatures. They had been a pain in his ass for more years than he could think about. And vampires. Blood-sucking animals that did nothing for the world in which they resided but fuck humans and drink from them.

Drain them. He thought that vampires should want to drain the human race. It would have gone a long way to helping him with his eradication of all human scum. But wolves could have been a part of his army had they not been so incredibly stupid.

"We have guests."

William turned to look at the man who had been serving him for nearly five decades.

"They wish a word with the man of the house."

"And what did they want with the man of the house, Timothy? Did they come to kill me in my own home?" William turned back to the formula he was preparing for when Ginger got there. He paused. "She's not coming. Not with Herman."

"I'm sorry, sir, what did you say?" Timothy looked at him oddly and William had the sudden urge to kill him. "Sir, the guest. What would you like for me to tell them?"

"Tell them? Tell them I don't give a good fuck what they want. I want them gone." As he turned back to the table he got a scent that he'd not smelled for a very long time. "Wolf."

Timothy backed up quickly. Even as he tripped up and fell backwards on the ground, he never stopped trying to get away. As soon as William stepped over him in his haste to get to his "guest," William paid him little mind. There was a wolf in his home. And he wanted to go out and kill him.

The great hall was empty of people. He raised his nose to the air and followed the scent of wolf until he found him in the living room. There were others there, but this was the one he wanted. This man of all men had been their downfall. Bernard Dublin had gotten messy and had cost them all.

"Do you know that she's near—" Dublin was clawing at his throat even as William came across the room at him. The harder he pinched his fingers, the harder Dublin struggled.

"You should have been dead. You said you had it under control. You said that you had everything under control." He let the man breathe for several seconds before he pinched again. "I should kill you where you stand, but I can't."

Dublin dropped to the floor and coughed. He didn't try to rise up, but lay where he was. William threw himself into a chair as the man across from him sat up then finally climbed into another chair. He was still coughing when Timothy brought him a drink as well as a wet cloth.

"I came to tell you…" He took several deep breaths. "I came to tell you that I have the right formula to make her eggs viable. The right combination of temperatures as well as the correct amount of magic. I've been working with some…" He looked around the room. "You do have her, don't you? You said you'd have her by now."

William roared again. This time, the only person who was terrified by it was his houseman Timothy. As soon as the door slammed behind him as he left the room, William got up and poured himself a large glass of wine. He didn't bother with the wolf because he wanted him dead.

"I'll have to go and retrieve her myself. She has been somewhat of a pain in the ass to find since you had to touch her that night." William had told him not to touch her, that she would see him for what he was, but the man was an idiot. "I've had to find her by other means. But some fucking wolf has stepped in and killed the one person I thought she trusted."

William had been assured that Dean Herman had her confidence. When he'd spoken to his wife, a woman of measurable talents, she'd told him that the girl had been sleeping with her husband for years. So much so that she'd left her husband because of the girl. William had thought he might have to go back and kill the wife of Herman just to see if she told the truth. But he'd let her live, thinking that he'd go back later and blame her death on her husband. After, of course, William killed him.

"We have to do something now. If we don't have her by the harvest moon, we may have to wait for another year before we can take her eggs. You know what the book said." William glared at Dublin.

"Yes, I know what the book said." He wanted to point out that he'd written the book over two hundred years ago as a lark, but didn't know how to explain that. As far as Dublin understood, William and he were the same age. "The book also says she must remain a virgin. How possible do you think that is in this day and age?"

"Quite good, as a matter of fact. You remember I know what she saw that night. I'm pretty sure that turned her off to sex forever." Dublin leaned back in his chair. "That was my plan all along."

William no more believed that than he did that Dublin wasn't still killing children. The man had a taste for it and as soon as this thing with his daughter was over with, he was going to kill him. William leaned back in his own chair and closed his eyes. He could never feel her, had never been able to touch Ginger's mind as he had hoped he would. Not once in all the time she'd been growing up.

His wife at the time had hated her. She had known that Ginger, they called her then, was going to have to go to each of the other's houses as soon as it could be arranged so that the council wouldn't find her. They knew about her, but not exactly where she was. It took a whole network of switching her around to keep her hidden. Then Dublin had touched Ginger and she'd read his mind. Then his cunt of a wife had called the cops and everything they had worked for fell to ribbons. Had William not had her taken to the orphanages that night then…

He looked over at Dublin. "How did you know where she was? The night of the party, you seemed to know where she was going to be taken. How did you know that?"

Dublin shifted in his chair and looked away. He was sure the man wasn't going to answer. When he did, William knew it was a lie.

"The cop. He told me. All of us, I think. Your wife said she was going to be taken there, didn't she?" He looked away with a little laugh. "I'm not sure after all this time how I found out. Why does it matter? Let's go and get her and harvest her."

William stood. Had he not needed the man he'd be dead. Smiling, he waved him toward the lab. They walked toward the area he'd had especially built and thought about the hundred ways he was going to kill this man. As soon as they walked into the lab William led him to the table. "You get started. I'll go and get her. I know just where she is." He knew that the pack house would be full of stupid wolves just like the one standing next to him. "As soon as I return, we will begin."

Dublin was already working on the formulas. As soon as William set one of his guards on Dublin, he left. He shifted as he tore through the house and was soaring into the night sky even as his clothes fell away to the ground.

The pack house was just where he thought it was. Deep into the wood and surrounded by forest. The leader had done well for himself, it seemed. He'd meant to come to the house sooner, meet with the man he would eventually kill, but had been caught up in the workings of his lab. Now he wished he'd have taken the time. Laid his plan better, got to know if the man was going to be a worthy, if slow-witted, adversary. He landed in a tree not far from the front of the house.

There was some activity going on, but not enough that he was worried. The man had done a great deal to fortify his compound. There was enough pack running around that William had to smile. They would be no match for him if he wanted to mow them down.

When the woman came out onto the porch and sat down William found himself moving closer to the earth to get a better look. She was lovely, in an older woman sort of way. He looked closer and saw that she was stringing beans, something he'd not seen anyone do in centuries. Shifting to mist, he moved closer to her.

She would do, he decided. He would take her in trade of the girl. He was just coming up on the porch when a small human, a child, came running out of the house. He froze her to the spot as he moved to the woman.

"You should know that they won't trade a broken down old woman for her."

William nodded, not caring that she could see him.

"They'll know that you have me. And when they come for you, they'll give you no mercy."

"I would expect no less. But the man inside has something that I want. And I believe you are wrong to think he would not trade…his mother." William knew in that moment that he would trade all for her. "You are but a pawn in this trade. I will have the girl."

She came to him without a fight. He was surprised by that and not entirely pleased. He wanted her to scream for him to let her go. He wanted her to bring the house out, have them find him with her. But no one stirred, not even the child when he let her go. When they were airborne, he sent a message through the child.

"You'll come with my property or I will kill the woman who gave you life. If you do not then I will take one person from you until I have what I want." The child went to the alpha, he knew. She would have no choice but to do as he bid. William could almost feel the girl in his possession again and nearly dropped the woman in his large claws.

"You will be well, my dear. Once I have gotten what I want and the alpha who dared to take from me is dead then I will think about letting you go." He smiled and looked at her. She didn't seem all that frightened of him and had a look of contentment on her face. "You don't seem concerned. Is there something I should know?"

"Oh yes. There is plenty you should know. But I've decided that I want to watch the things unfold that kills you."

He didn't know why, but that gave him a slight tremor of fear. He'd not felt that emotion in so long that he'd nearly forgotten what it was. William wanted her to suffer and dropped her nearly too far from the ground when he reached the clearing by his lab and home. When he picked her up after shifting, he knew that she was broken and would be lucky if she could make it tomorrow. But she only smiled at him and closed her eyes. William had her taken to the lab right away and tried to forget her. She was not so easily dismissed.

CHAPTER 14

No one in the house moved. Luna had told them what she had heard and had sat down and fell asleep. Austin got up to pick her up and then sat with her in his arms. Connor wasn't sure what he needed to do, but sitting here was not helping their mother.

"What does he think this is going to do? Does he expect us to just give her over as if she isn't a member of this family?" Austin didn't seem to be asking anyone the question so no one answered. "I wouldn't do that even if she hit me with that spoon of hers repeatedly. She's my mom, for Christ's sake."

"I have to go to him. If I don't then he will kill your mom."

Connor stood up when Lou did.

"I go alone. I have to find—"

"You and I go together or no one leaves. We are pack now. You and I are mates now. *We* go to find her and bring her home."

"And if either of you think you're leaving this house without all of us then you're fucking insane. But we need a plan. We can't just go there willy-nilly and expect to come out the—"

"Did you just say willy-nilly?" Connor looked at his other family then back at Austin. "Please tell me that I heard you wrong. Big, bad alpha Austin Jefferson Force said willy-nilly?"

"I'm trying to project a better image. So fuck the hell off." He glared at his mate then looked at Connor again. "You wait until you have a cub or two. Then you'll think differently when the first word they say is 'fuck it.'"

Connor stared at him for all of ten seconds before he burst out laughing. He could see it now, little Austin or Nancy walking around the house saying just that and Austin and CJ trying to tell them not to. He had to sit down and pulled Lou into his lap. This was just too great. Then he thought of his mom. "She will be pissed if we get hurt. I mean. really pissed. She might hit all of us with her spoon." Connor nodded to the one sitting on the table between them. "I'm going to take her that one when we get her." He picked it up and put in on Lou's lap. After they had returned from the mall, they told them all what had happened. Well, most of it. He kissed Lou's shoulder and nodded to the rest of them.

"We know where the lab is. I've been there before when we first moved here. After Lou told me what she'd seen in her dream, I knew just where it was." He looked over at Gordon. "You remember the place? It's near the old homestead about ten miles from here. Remember about six months ago when someone told us it had been sold?"

"Yeah. I remember. Some company…let me see." Gordon got up and went to the office only to return in a few minutes. He had a file in his hand. "Here it is. I thought the name was strange then, but now that I see the whole… Here you go, Lou. What do you think?"

Shadowgram. It was an old word that he'd heard before, something his grandmother had said about photographs. He looked at Lou when she stiffened. She knew something and he was willing to bet that it wasn't good news.

"I remember from the touch of Dublin that he was saying this word over and over. I didn't know what it meant, but I had…" She looked up at him. "They're going to make more of him, remember me telling you that? Well, I'm pretty sure that I'm the oven."

The room was incredibly quiet. Then when CJ started laughing, everyone stared at her. It took her several moments to get herself under control enough to tell them what she thought was so funny.

"Don't you see? He thinks that you're still human." Before anyone could comment, she continued. "It won't work now. You're wolf. And from all the history that I've read and from what I know, there is no viable way for it to ever come to be. Wolf eggs can only be fertilized by another wolf and then it has to be a mate."

Connor looked at Lou. Was it that simple? Probably, but that didn't mean that he wasn't going to kill the bastard. He'd taken his mother, harmed his mate. There was no way this prick was going to walk away from this clean. He started to say that when Phil spoke.

"There is something else that we have to figure on. This man has been using a lot of magic. Most of it is black and therefore unstable, but he would have had to have had a bit of his own before. The reason we need to consider all this is because he isn't going to be alone. There will be others, none as powerful as him, there as well and they'll want a piece of her."

"What do you think we should do?"

Everyone looked at Hope.

"I know you have a plan. I've not been your mother for over four hundred years without knowing that look."

"I think we should take the fight to our own grounds. Bring him here." Austin looked like he was going to protest when Phil held up his hand. "Think about it. The caves are going to be hard enough for us to get around. At least here we know the property and the land. We also have an advantage that he isn't aware of."

Everyone waited, but nothing was forthcoming. Finally, Holly slapped him on the shoulder and told him to behave. "You jerk, tell them, will you?"

"We have her."

Everyone looked at Lou. She flushed in Connor's arms and then shook her head. "Me? I don't have anything near what he might have. And you said yourself he has black magic. All I have is a little ability to see things."

"And with that, we can find him. You've touched something of his, correct?"

She started to shake her head and then nodded.

"Where is it?"

She held up the opener she'd picked up at the mall. "I don't know why I picked it up in the first place. But it seemed so out of place lying there among the empty cans and blood."

Phil stepped toward her and then stopped just short of taking it from her. "Read it. You know you know how. Simply tell us what you see when you read it."

"I don't know if…what if I can't? What if it has nothing to do with anything?"

Phil shook his head.

"Then you touch it."

"If I do then you won't be able to get anything from it and you know it." He knelt in front of her. "You only have to do what comes natural to you. Read it. Let yourself go and see what you can find out about the man who is going to try and destroy us."

Connor was afraid for her and really didn't want her to do it. He knew when she looked at him she was asking him, but he knew that she had to make this decision on her own. He also thought that in addition to that, she needed to know that she could do this for them. "You can do this. We both know that you can. But if you don't want to or are afraid, that'll be all right as well." He nodded to the opener. "Something made you pick that up. Maybe that's what it was. Another thought to the end of this prick."

She nodded. And looked around the room. "I don't know if this will help or not, but if you'll all…please don't judge me if this thing tells me what we need."

Austin snorted. "You're Connor's mate. If we were going to judge you, it would be on your choice of mate, not what you can do. Do it, kid, and we'll be right there with you."

When she took it out of her pocket he noticed that there was blood on it. He wondered if that might hurt her chances, but didn't have a clue. When she sat on the floor in front of the fireplace he started toward her.

She shook her head. "No. I can't think if you touch me. I need to have space. Someone will…I don't always remember what happens so someone should take notes."

"You talk and we'll get it. We're right here for you." CJ sat down with a pen and a notebook. "You might not be able to read it when I'm done, but we'll have it."

After nodding again, she held the simple metal can opener to her head. She closed her eyes and took a deep breath. When she opened them again a few seconds later he knew that she was no longer in the room with them, but somewhere else. Christ, it worked.

"The place he lives is over a large lab. There is enough equipment in the room to do experiments on several thousand species. But he only has one in mind. He wants the girl Ginger Louise."

~~~

They had a plan. She wasn't thrilled with it, but they had one. Lou rolled to her back and looked up at the ceiling. Connor had brought her up here after she'd finished with the reading. He told her he'd be right back and for her to rest.

"How the hell am I supposed to rest when he's gone?" She hadn't realized she'd spoken out loud until her voice startled her into laughter. "Stupid man. Why doesn't he come back here and relax me a little bit more?"

"Are you talking to yourself?"

She looked up when he spoke. She'd not heard him come in.

"Should I go out and let you finish?"

She started to glare at him and decided to have a little fun. "You could, I suppose. I think I can handle what I need done on my own." She pulled the sheet down off her body and stretched. "Hummm, I'm thinking I could give myself as much pleasure as you can."

She heard the door shut and the lock click home. She didn't hear him move so assumed that he was still near the door. She glanced up at him to see him standing close to the bed. He looked…well, hungry came to mind.

"Show me. Show me what sort of pleasure you can give yourself."

She looked up at him and didn't move.

"Show me, Lou. Show me what you need."

She didn't have a clue, but if he continued to look at her like that she'd figure something out. Moving her hand over her breast she heard a low groan and was surprised to realize it was her.

Her nipples were so responsive that she found she wanted to touch them. Sliding up her shirt, she cupped both hands around her breasts and lifted them up. She closed her eyes and thought about his mouth on her, suckling her.

"I love the way your mouth takes me in. When you bite at my nipples, it's nearly enough to make me come." She rolled her hips up and decided she wanted to be naked in the worst way. Reaching down to the zipper on her pants, she pulled the tab down with one hand and tweaked her nipple with the other. "When I touch me this way, I can feel it all the way to my toes."

He growled. It was low and long and she looked up at him. His grip on the bed post looked painful and she wondered if there would be marks from his nails when he let it go. That turned her on more and she found she wanted to see him lose control. Moving to take off her pants, she asked him not to move until she said he could.

"You're playing with fire. Do you have any idea what it's doing to me to watch you play?"

She nodded.

"Then you'd better enjoy this because when I'm allowed to touch you I'm going to take you hard."

"You promise?" He nodded and she noticed that his arms were tight. He looked like something ready to spring. She moved to take off her pants completely then her shirt and bra. She left her panties on as much for herself as him.

"You smell like sex."

She touched her nipples again and danced her hips on the bed, never taking her eyes off of him.

"You smell like the promise of fulfillment."

"I don't really know what to do." She sounded frustrated even to her own ears. "Tell me what to do. Tell me what you'd like for me to do."

"Touch yourself. I want to see you slide your fingers into your wet pussy and ride them. Then I want you to feed the juices to me."

She moaned and did as he asked.

"That's it, baby. Touch your heat."

Her fingers slid into her slick opening. She moaned every time she touched her clit, but didn't let herself come. When she felt she was covered enough, she lifted her trembling fingers to his mouth and he suckled them in. Her climax ripped from her.

"Again. Come again." She rode her other hand as he licked her clean. The second time she came, she cried out his name and he dropped to his knees beside her, but didn't touch. "You're killing me. Spread your legs and let me drink from you. Please, baby, I need to taste all that heat."

She moved to the center of the bed and he settled between her legs. Pulling her ass to the edge, she sat up on her elbows as he moved closer to her. When he wrapped his hands into her panties, she was panting as hard as he was.

"When you come, I'm going to let my wolf have a taste of you too. I'm going to let him have his fill of you before I take you."

She nodded, uncaring how he made her his, just so long as he did it. "Then I want to take you from behind and fuck you until you scream out my name."

"Please. Hurry ple—" His tongue filled her. When he touched the spot inside of her, she screamed. Not his name, but close enough. His finger spread her and when he took her clit and soft lips into his mouth and nipped at her, she came up off the bed with another scream. Every time he commanded her to come again, she did, her body responding to his as if he owned it. She supposed he did.

When she lay limp on the bed, just short of begging him to stop, he stood up. He was stripped down to his bare skin in seconds. When he stood over her with his fist around his cock she thought he was the most beautiful creature in the world.

"You asked for this. But now…now I want it to be better for us. I want to make love to you."

She nodded, not really understanding the difference. She wanted him now.

Before she could tell him anything, he had her move to the center of the bed and he followed her. When she was settled, he sat between her thighs and looked down at her.

"Tomorrow, we're going to go into the lion's den and I want to remember you just like this when I look at that prick I'm going to kill." He leaned down and kissed her nipple gently. "Then when he's lying there bleeding, I'm going to tell him why I killed him."

Another kiss to her other nipple. She was thinking because of his mom, but she was wrong.

"I'm going to tell him that he shouldn't have fucked with my mate."

When he moved over her this time, he took her mouth. Not in a kiss that she expected, but a gentle one. One that said love and respect, a kiss that told her that he cherished her and he loved her. When the tears threatened, she moved to touch his face and he leaned into it. She kissed him back as softly and with as much love as he had shown her.

When he slid into her, she moaned. It was a fulfillment of his love, not sex. She wrapped her legs around him and canted up. She wanted him deep inside of her. Moving with his every stroke, her climax built. Built to a point where she wasn't sure she would survive when she did come.

He nipped at her shoulder then. His teeth grazed at her flesh in a way that asked for permission rather than taking. When he tilted her head back and gave him her throat he moaned and when he bit her she cried out, not in pain, but because she loved him. Connor Force could not have claimed her in any other way than he did. His own climax was beautiful to her, gave her such hope and love that she cried again when he held her tightly.

"I love you, Lou. I will love you for the rest of our days." He pulled her body over his and held her. "There will be so much we will be able to do once this is over, and I want to start a life with you at my side."

Snuggling deep into his body, she nodded. "And I love you as well. Once this is over, I plan to show you daily. Hourly."

His even breathing told her he slept and she was lulled into it with him by the tick of his heart beating. Thinking about the next day didn't bother her so much now. She had the love of a great man and one that would be by her no matter what.

CHAPTER 15

Nancy knew that she was hurt, but not how badly. When the man had taken her, she could only think about the little girl Luna and not what he might have planned for her. The stupid man was going to pay for taking her. She just hoped that none of her family was hurt in the process. She tried to sit up again.

The pain was dizzying. She knew that she had at least some ribs broken and from the way it hurt to breathe, she was thinking all of them. She smiled. She knew also that her arm was broken and thought about shifting, but didn't want to be caught in a place that would render her unable to protect herself if need be.

When she heard the scraping of the little man coming back she lay down and closed her eyes. The last time he was here he had fussed about her so much that she'd wanted to scream. But he had left her with some water and a washcloth. She watched him enter the cell and close the door behind him. This time he had a tray and what smelled to her like a first aid kit.

"I can't believe he'd do this to a woman of your station. To think that I would…well, he will just need to get over the fact that I'm not going to let her die." Nancy was still trying to figure out what station he was referring to when he came close enough for her to touch. "Miss, are you awake?"

"I hurt." The words slipped out before she could stop them. He touched her ribs and sent a searing pain through her body. "Please, just go away."

"I cannot, my lady. Not knowing that you hurt as you do." He moved away then came back with the tray. "I have brought you some broth. As well as something for the pain. I wouldn't suggest that you shift, though I know it will make you feel better because of the magic held here. He will surely find out, and when he does I don't believe I will be able to help you."

He moved the tray closer to where she lay and sat on the cold ground. She stared at him when he held up a spoon with steaming liquid toward her. She didn't know how stupid he thought she was, but she wasn't going to—

Just then he took the spoon to his mouth and ate from it. He swallowed then stuck out his tongue to show her that he'd actually eaten it. She laughed despite the situation. "You think that proves anything? I used to do the same for my children when they didn't like dinner. Of course I would spit it out of my cheeks when they weren't looking. But that's beside the point." He smiled at her and gave her another bite of soup. She took it this time without hesitation. "Where are we?"

"In the cave above your home. I see you there. Well, not you, but the pack. You have a very lovely one." He fed her several more bites before he wiped off her mouth. "If your family comes for you, he will kill them."

"He'll try." She leaned back and closed her eyes. "What does he want with them? Why is he pursuing my family?"

"The girl. I don't know her name, but he is and has been obsessed with her for years. When she first disappeared he was livid for nearly a decade. He'd find trails of her, but never her. He wants her for unspeakable things." He looked away before continuing. "The man, Dublin, he means to keep her for himself after he tries to kill my master."

146

Nancy thought about that. She knew what her family had found out, but that was so very little considering what he must know about them. She looked at the man when he stood up. He smiled again and it looked so sad on him. She asked him what his name was.

"I started out as simply 'boy.' Then as the years passed, I became 'servant,' then 'you.' After a while, someone asked my name. I told him it was Timothy. That is what I go by now." He smiled again, sadder this time. "It doesn't matter what anyone calls me. I shall be dead long before this is over."

"Why is that?" He put the first aid kit near her, as well as an unopened bottle of pain reliever. He moved toward the door, this time leaving the key in the lock on her side. "Timothy?"

"He is busy in the lower chambers now. Well below where you are. If one were to go to the right, they would see the opening out. To the left, they would be able to see the door that locks the lower levels from this side." He nodded toward the box. "Inside there is all you will need. Everything. But do be careful and fruitful when you use it."

"I would like for you to come with me. When I leave, I would very much like for you to come as well." He shook his head. "Why not? Do you owe him so much?"

"I owe him nothing, but we are attached. When he goes, so shall I." He nodded again toward the kit on the floor. "It will be the only thing that saves you."

Then he was gone.

Nancy crawled to the smallish box, her body not nearly as pain filled as it had been. By the time she got to it, she was hurting, but breathing and moving much easier. When she pulled it into her lap, she opened it and looked inside. She lay back against the wall just behind her and thought of what Timothy had done for her. She picked up one of the items in the box, the cell phone, and dialed out. The first person who answered was her son Connor.

"Mom?" He might have said more, but she cut him off. She had no idea how much time she had before he figured it out, nor did she know if the signal would hold. She told him where she was and that she was going to be alright.

"The man is going to kill us all if given the chance. I want you to work together to bring him down." She closed her eyes again, hoping she wasn't sending her children into certain death. "I will be waiting outside the entrance for you then we'll go in and take his ass down. Understand?"

"Yes. Mom, please tell me that you're alright. I don't want...Luna said he snatched you from the chair without touching you."

She nodded, then remembered he couldn't see her. "He did. But I believe I have something that'll help us. Something that I think must belong to Lou." She picked up the key, not knowing why she thought it belonged to the child. "Ask her about a key. Ask her if she remembers what it might go to." She heard Connor ask someone and assumed it was Lou. When she got on the phone, Nancy had to smile. The girl was ten kinds of pissed.

"You have like ten minutes to talk to your children and you ask me about a key. What the hell, woman, don't you want to ask how they are? What they're going to do to get your ass home?"

Nancy laughed then caught her breath on the pain.

Lou heard her. "Of all the...yes, I remember a key. I had it with me the night that my parents threw me under the bus. I don't know what it was for or where it went."

"I have it." Nancy waited for her to say something, anything, but she didn't. In that moment she knew that Lou knew where the key went. "Can you use it to take this sucker out of our lives so that I can hold my grandchildren again?"

"He won't go easy. Not even with…where did you get it?"

Nancy looked to the opened door and then at the kit on her lap.

"Was it a short man with graying hair and a very polite way about him?"

"Timothy, yes. Do you know him?" Lou said she did. "He is helping me get away so that you can come and rescue me."

"He was the other cop. He took the key from me that night. He pulled me aside and told me that he would keep it safe, thus keeping me safe. I had forgotten about it and him until just now."

Nancy was going to find the man and make him come with them. "Come and get me and this key. I want this man stopped today."

"So do I, Mrs. Force. So do I."

The line went dead and she closed the phone. It was just as well. For whatever reason, she knew it was time for her to get going. Putting the long chain around her neck, she put it and the key under her shirt. She was moving toward the door when she grabbed the last item in the box.

She had no idea where the map was supposed to lead them, but she wasn't leaving what might be her only weapon. Holding it like it was her lifeline, Nancy made a left hand turn and locked the door to the sublevels. When she was finished she turned and made her way to the surface to wait for her children to come and save the day.

~~~

It only took them twenty minutes to get to where the cave was. But it seemed like several lifetimes. Lou moved up the mountain just behind the men and in front of CJ. Holly had been left at home under a great deal of protest to watch after the children. Phil had told her if she moved off the couch he was going to drain her.

Lou smiled, thinking that the man looked positively in love with his mate. He'd kissed their unborn child twice before he simply turned into a steel man and walked out of the room. His entire body had become incased in silver in less than a heartbeat. Lou had looked at Holly before she could speak.

"It's a part of his birthright. Don't touch him. He'll kill anyone who touches him that is not his mate." Holly grinned. "He does get all medieval when he wants to, doesn't he?"

She stopped when the wolves in front of her did. She still couldn't believe that she was a wolf and that these people were as well. When Connor slid up next to her and nuzzled her neck she growled low and stepped closer to him.

"You're killing me right now. I know that my mom needs me, but all I can think of is how simply beautiful you are."

She whimpered and sent him her love.

"Don't get hurt. I will beat your ass if you do."

"You either. And for the record, I need your mom too." She looked up when one of the others started to growl softly. *"I think they found her."* Everyone shifted and pulled on clothes, only just enough to cover what was necessary. They knew that when they went in, they would have to shift again.

Nancy looked good. Very good as a matter of fact, and when she showed her the key that she had on Lou didn't know what to think. She looked up at Austin when he stalked toward her.

"Will it work to do whatever we need to get rid of this man?"

She nodded.

"Good. Then you lead the way. And you'd better not get yourself hurt, or so help me, I'll sic CJ on you."

The snort behind her made her think it was CJ and she was laughing. Lou turned to Connor to see what he thought of his brother's declaration. He nodded at her then stood beside her as they shifted once again.

They moved almost as one into the mouth of the cave. Nancy was with them as a wolf this time and it surprised Lou that she could see gray around her muzzle and along her fur. She moved slowly, like she was in some pain, but not as much as Lou thought she really was. It took them less than ten minutes to get to the opening and only a minute or two before they found the body of who Nancy said was Tim.

"He killed himself." Nancy stood over him for several minutes and seemed so sad. The man had taken a gun to his head. Lou had a feeling that he had done it to avoid being killed by his master. She hoped that none of them would wish the same thing before this was over.

There were nearly two hundred of them strong. Phil was with them, but he was shadowed so that he could remain in his armor. He had several men with him, all vampires that he said he trusted. One of them was Myles, the man from the hospital.

The other wolves were peeling off from the larger body and going down off-shoots of the long hall. Several went up the stairs and even more moved through the other rooms as silently as a breeze. By the time they got to the locked lab door, every part of the upper levels had been thoroughly searched and anyone in the house was taken away quickly. When they stood before the door Nancy showed them where she'd hidden the key that Timothy had given her. The key to the rooms that the lab was behind.

As Phil stepped forward to turn the lock, Nancy reached for her. *"You'll be safe or I'll do far worse than my son will to you. I know that you carry his child."* Lou turned to look at her. *"I'm not as stupid as some of them think I am."*

"I doubt very much that any of them think you're stupid. Not to mention, they're all terrified of you." Lou moved into the room ahead of the others as she continued. *"Then there is the fact that I need you to show me how to be a mom. I've never had any experience worth snot with the job requirements."*

"Deal. But you must promise me one thing."

Lou hesitated for several seconds waiting for her to tell her.

"You must let Connor make you as happy as you have him."

Lou turned to look at her while everyone in the pack froze. The bond that formed between the two of them in that moment Lou knew would last several lifetimes. With a quick nod, she turned and moved to the labs. The first person they came upon was Dublin.

The plan was simple enough. Move in, kill them all, then blow the place up before they left. She moved up behind Dublin and shifted to herself. She reached for the gown lying on the table next to him before he turned. He looked surprised, yes, but she also saw the fear written in his eyes.

"Do you know who I am?"

He shook his head then peered at her closer before he suddenly nodded.

"Do you know why I'm here?"

"I would presume to kill me. That's not going to be nearly as easy as you might think." He leaned in and sniffed her before he stepped back. "You're a wolf too. Oh that's rich. William isn't going to be happy about that one bit. But I don't think it'll matter in the long run."

"And why is that?" She watched the others move about the room until Dublin was surrounded. "Did you think I'd just let him do what he wanted to me and not put up a fight?"

"Oh, I hope you fight. I haven't had a good tussle with anyone in a few days." He reached out to touch her cheek and she stepped back. His laughter made her mad, but she didn't move. "You're nothing like he thinks you are, are you?"

"Nor you." She felt the shift race up her arm and to her hand. Before he could move to grab for her, she reached her clawed hand out and tore his throat out. He grabbed at his ruined flesh and started choking. "I'm not four anymore."

He dropped to the floor where he stood, his blood staining the floor beneath him. She stepped over his dying body and moved toward the only other door in the room. Before she got to it Austin was standing in front of her.

"Are you hurt?"

She looked at him oddly before shaking her head.

"Good. You do something like that again without my permission and I will punish you beyond your wildest thoughts. Do I make myself clear?"

She nodded and stepped up to him. "You don't know what he did to me all those years ago."

"And you don't have any right to murder without cause." Before he could move away, she reached out and grabbed his arm. She sent him every thought, every dream of what Dublin had done to all the children that had been put into his care and what he'd done to the little bodies when he was finished with them.

He staggered back and held onto the wall. She hadn't thought of what she'd done to him, only pissed that he felt she had no right. When he reached out to her again, she nearly buckled at the knees when he wiped a tear from his cheek as he touched hers.

"I'm so sorry. I had no idea that he'd... You knew, didn't you? All along, you knew that he was a monster." He moved behind her and she nearly shifted again when he continued. "Thank you, Lou."

They moved slowly into the bowels of the earth to confront the man who had hurt so many. The lab was running, machines were doing their jobs, but William was nowhere in sight.

CHAPTER 16

He could smell them. William didn't know how many came, but he could smell wolf and vampire. Packing up the notes he'd taken over the past years, he moved to the wall to hide away. He was just closing the door behind him when she walked in.

William wanted to go out and inspect her. He nearly had when he saw the others with her. He had a thought that she was the alpha, but as soon as the monster of a wolf that had come in behind her spoke to them, he knew the alpha. However, he was mesmerized by her even as she shifted to human again.

She was a wolf. He had no idea how that had happened as they had taken out her ability to shift when she'd been created. Or so Dublin had told him. He glanced up at the door and wondered if he could even now go up and kill the fat wolf, but decided that if he tried he was going to be hurt.

"I know you're in here. I can smell your vile stench." Even her voice was something to marvel at. There was so much command in it he was impressed with her. "Come out now and I'll kill you quickly."

He wanted to laugh at her. Bigger men, even older wizards had tried to kill him, yet here he was to prove that he was of a superior race. He willed the containers around the room to explode, trying to kill off some of the men that had dared come with her. He didn't hear anyone howl in pain.

"My name is Austin Jackson Force. I am pack alpha to these men and women and also high Trustee of the Council for Vampires and Wolves. I hereby order you to come from where you are and be sentenced."

William laughed quietly. The man was positively entertaining. Using very little of his magic, he reached out to the room in general and answered the obtuse man. He was still laughing when he spoke. "Threaten me? Why you stupid dog. Do you have any idea what I have of yours? Do you only now see what power I have? Don't be ignorant. Leave the girl with Dublin and I shall think about letting you live until I finish with her. She means nothing to you and everything to me." William waited for the room to clear. When he could still feel them in his lab, he leaned his head against the door to listen and was surprised by the laughter.

"You want me, big boy, then you can come out and try your best to get me."

William's head popped back so quickly that he hit it on the wall behind him. Her voice did not sound respectful at all.

"Do you hear me, old man? Come out and show us just what a coward you really are."

He was nearly ready to do so when he heard her laugh again.

"Oh and by the way, Dublin is dead. I killed him myself. Tore his useless throat from him like he was warmed cheese. Oh, and I have my mother-in-law too." Her laugher rang through to him. "You aren't such a big bad ass at all, are you?"

He had to take several deep breaths before he would allow himself to speak. The girl was going to pay. He was going to make her suffer in ways that… He suddenly realized what she had said. Dublin was dead. If he was dead then… "I don't believe you have the nerve to kill one of mine. Do you know what the consequences are for killing a wolf? There are rules governing that sort of thing." He knew there were. He'd been breaking those rules for all his life. "How do I know that you don't lie?"

"Because I don't. You want to know then you're going to have to grow some balls and come out of hiding. You know, I didn't know little men like you could be so afraid of a woman that you'd hide in a closet like a little girl."

He didn't like what she was saying and reached for the small mechanism in the door to open it. There was nothing there.

He frantically searched for the small lock and nearly sent himself into a panic when his fingers finally touched it. He heard some noises, but was more concerned with teaching the bitch a lesson than revealing where he was hiding. As soon as the door opened he froze in his spot.

The lab was destroyed. Not just the equipment, though that was bad enough, but everything looked like it had been melted down and now pooled on the floor in large puddles of steel. There were hundreds of eyes staring back at him, more than he could count right now. He looked around at the devastation and then at the girl who stood in the middle of it all. "What have you done?" His breath was nearly knocked out of him from the impact of the room. "You can't have done this all on your own."

"And why is that? Because I'm a woman and so beneath your abilities? Or is it because you don't think anyone but you has any magic?" She made a sound much like a machine when it is done with a cycle. "Wrong. I might be a bit less controlled about what I can do, but I'm no less…powerful."

He moved, not toward her, but what was once his table. He looked at the glass and metal twisted together and the lump of what could only be the steel table. He moved to other items he'd been using not minutes before, all them broken, twisted, and now a mess on the floor.

The walls had fared no better. What had once been glass cubicles that stood alone to give his workers the opportunity to work independently or with a group now lay in an artistic grouping that resembled a glassed Jackson Pollack painting rather than the pristine walls he'd spared no expense on to make this project work. She stood in the middle of the room that he only just realized was empty save for the two of them.

"You're not alone."

She shook her head and smiled. He would have said it was a scary smile rather than one of friendliness.

"Do you have any idea who I am to you?"

"Yes, I know what you think you are to me. I also know your every thought." She slid into his mind as easily as he had killed a man who had defied him. He saw what she'd done to Dublin and had to grasp the closest object to hang onto. It just happened to be the wall.

"No. No, you lie." Her smile said she did not. "I'm much more powerful than you'll ever be."

"Yeah, about that. I don't want to be the all-powerful Oz. I want to be Lou Force, mate to Connor Force. But I can't do that." She crossed her arms over her chest and glared at him. "Do you want to know why?"

He didn't really. How could something so perfect turn so quickly? He looked around the room for something, anything, that he could use to toss at her. She laughed a little and he looked back at her.

"I have the key."

He staggered this time. She knew entirely too much. Timothy was going to—

"He's dead. By his own hand, but only because you drove him to it. It's just one more death to add to your growing number of crimes."

He reached for the man and found the connection not only lost, but severed. He reached harder and found him with his brain on the wall behind him and the gun still in his hands. He'd actually gone and done it. Killed himself rather than serve him for the rest of his days. "He was worthless. He was a constant source of amusement to me and I only allowed him to hang around for that value alone." He was reaching and stalling. He didn't like to be reduced to do either. "I should thank you for telling me where he is."

"No need. Nancy appreciated him more in the last hour of his death than you probably did his entire life. Sad but true." She laughed without humor. "You could say that he's the real reason we're all here."

They appeared then. Only a few at first then a few more as time seemed to slow down around him. He didn't let go of the wall, but continued to hang onto it. He didn't like the fact that he needed the support, but there was no way he was going to look weak in front of her either. He'd been the most powerful being in the universe for nearly a thousand years. One snippet of a girl, one of his creations, was not going to take that from him so easily. He was startled out of his anger when she spoke.

"I said, you didn't answer my question."

He looked at her trying to remember what she had posed before him.

"You didn't ask why I can't simply be Lou Force. Don't you care to see that your monster is happy? You really should ask me."

"Monster? What is that? You're no more a monster than—" William stopped talking when the wolf at her side growled low. There was saliva hanging from his muzzle and his eyes looked red, evil red. "Is that supposed to be your mate? He looks worthless."

Her laughter made his skin crawl. She was very good at this, too good at making terror run along his skin like a thousand bugs. He rubbed his arms without thought and raised his chin when she laughed again.

"Yes, he is. The man that I love. And he's taken exception to the fact that you were about to say I'm no more a monster than you are. But back to the reason I can't be Lou Force. I don't think I ever want to be called her again because like Ginger, that name brings me bad memories. From now on, I want to be called Louise Force. The woman I was always meant to be. " She took a step toward him then another as she continued. "As for you being a monster? We both know that you're precisely that, a monster. But we're going to take care of that soon enough. Any last thoughts?"

He couldn't believe this was happening. Did she honestly think that she could take him out? Apparently, that's exactly what she thought. He looked at the wolves as they moved with her. As a pack, he supposed, but more like a well-planned dance. Each of her steps that brought her closer to him also brought the horde of wolves too.

William reached for the magic that surrounded the lab, the mountain as well as the earth even beyond that. There was more there than he'd ever be able to use. Certainly more than he'd need to kill off a pack of wolves and take his prize. As he pulled it to him, he felt it build. Looking at her, he could see no fear, but knew that soon that would change as well. "No. I have no last words other than to tell you that you are going to regret this a great deal more than any of them." William released a bit of the magic hiding his true self from her. "They will be dead momentarily, and you? You will be mine."

The magic slid from his hand and toward the girl. She was smiling again, but he knew what it was—a sham. She was going to pay for this. Pay for all of this. He threw back his head and laughed when it hit his target.

~~~

Terror made her stiffen, but she didn't move. She couldn't move without harming the others. She only hoped that this worked. If it didn't then she was going to kill that fucking man who had talked her into this. If she lived.

The power drifted around her just as he said it would. She stood still, waiting for the signal to move. When none came, she nearly moved forward to take out the bastard who had hurt so many. But the small voice beside her made her still again.

"I think if you move, I will personally kick your ass. What part of 'don't move no matter what goes on around you' did you not understand?"

She wanted to hit him.

"If you do then you'll be moving and, again, that's what you're not supposed to do."

"He thinks he's won." She could see William even as the dark magic dissipated around her. *"The next time he tries this, you might not be able to protect us all."*

"You doubt me?" Phil snorted. *"I am the...what did you call yourself? Ah yes, the all-powerful Oz. Well, kiddo, I am him and a little bit more. Stand still before I have to sic Connor on you."*

She wanted to look at Connor, but just refrained from doing so. He was near her, she could feel him. When he moved slightly against her leg, she felt a great deal better. He licked along her hand and she curled her fingers around the contact.

"Better?"

She nodded, knowing he could see her.

"Good. Remember what I told you. Keep talking to him until the rest of the council has a chance to see what he is. With that information, it will make taking him out easier. Just a little more time is all they need."

She'd agreed to this plan hours ago. She had been told that without that vital information, they wouldn't be able to subdue him, much less kill him. Lou had thought that by now, someone would have been able to tell them that he was an evil prick and would have him dead. Phil laughed. She knew he was reading her thoughts and while she wasn't happy about it, she knew that right now it was the only thing keeping her alive.

"Nancy is healed and is waiting with my mate. You should also know that there are a number of men working on yours and Connor's home to get it finished. I'm thinking that as soon as we leave here, you'll be picking carpet swatches and curtain patterns."

"I don't care about that shit." She glanced over at Connor when she was sure he'd laughed. *"I don't even care that we have a house."*

He was trying to distract her. She knew this, and allowed him to do it. By now William was looking at all of them as if he couldn't understand what the fuck had just happened.

"You're not dead."

She wanted to laugh at his tone, but didn't move.

"You should be...all of them should be dead and you should be laying there writhing in pain and begging me to make you better."

"I heal quickly. Do you?" She didn't expect an answer so wasn't surprised that none was forthcoming. The small move again made her take two steps forward before she was told to stop. "Do you heal quickly like a vamp or like a wolf? Like me."

"Wolf?" He seemed to spit out the word. "Useless animals that I plan to kill right along with every human in this world. Do you have any idea how long I've been putting up with Dublin? Decades. And the dog wasn't even house trained."

When he didn't continue, she asked again, "So you're vampire? Figures. All the blood-sucking things do is order you about and expect you to bow—"

"Vampire? Not all of me. I do have a bit of them running through my veins, but not entirely." He raised his hands again and she knew he was gathering more magic to try and hurt them. "What other creatures do you know? Surely there is something you can think of that is more powerful than a vampire or a dog?"

She didn't have any idea and reached gently into his mind. There was information there. A great deal of it, but what he was seemed to be elusive.

He might have blocked her, but she was quicker. Every time he tried to push her out of his mind she simply went around him. She had been doing this a long time, mostly to protect herself from monsters like him, but also to see what harm the person could cause her.

"You won't find it with your silly attempts at mind raping me." He laughed and she could see a dark ball of something building in his hands. He was going to throw that at her, she just knew it. "You should really give up. If you don't, then I may have to hurt you in ways that will make my need for you simply out of the question."

She was nearly ready to pull out when she touched something that made him cringe. She moved around the object he put in front of her, memories of something he'd done, a child that he'd thought was her and who he'd killed. She tried to ignore the pain he was making her feel when she found the string. Then another. Then another as she got closer to what he didn't want anyone to know about him. As soon as she touched it, she turned to Phil and smiled. "He's a dragon."

The room seemed to explode with beings. There were nearly fifty wolves in the room with her, all of them pack and a dozen vampires, all of them on the council or a part of it somehow. But as soon as she said dragon, thirty more or so came into the room, all of them bent on taking the being down in front of her. She stopped them with a single word.

"I would very much like to speak to him once more before you sentence him."

Hope Campbell looked at her then nodded to the men who right now were wrapping William in some sort of netting. She supposed it was something made especially to hold him.

"Why?"

He didn't answer her, but continued to struggle. When he did, she could see the madness in his face.

"Why did you create me? What did you hope to gain?"

"Gain? Why, do you have any idea what people would pay to see a real dragon? Not one like me. I'm not what they want, but one that I was planning to make with your eggs? One that would not only do my bidding, but would make me more than rich, more than well known; it would make me everything."

She stepped back when he moved toward her, even with the netting. "You could have been so much without all this magic. A wonder to the world. Why didn't you just let things be?"

He lunged at her this time and had dislodged the men holding him. As he was making good his escape, she ran after him. They were nearly to the door when she leapt at him, hoping that she could knock him away enough that the others, the ones that had the netting, could get a grasp on him again. She knew that if he were able to gather more magic that this time, there would be no saving any of them. Lou knew then without a doubt that this one was big enough to take them all out. Her wolf clawed along her skin and Lou let her come out.

She cried out and felt the wolf, her wolf, cry out as well. Then before she could get away or stop him, she heard a scream that would haunt her for the rest of her life. It sounded like someone was dying. And she was afraid it was her.

CHAPTER 17

The spoon lay beside him on the chair. The funeral was set to start in ten minutes, but he couldn't seem to stop staring at it. He looked up at his brother Austin as well as CJ when they sat in the chair on the opposite side of the wooden spoon. Both of them looked back at it before they spoke.

"There are more people here than I thought there would be. I mean, I wasn't sure that anyone would come at all." Austin nodded to the small and large groups of people standing around talking as he continued. "Do you think any of them are here for the service, or is it something else?"

"They're here for us. They like us." Connor watched a smaller group turn into a much larger one when some of the pack joined. "They all seem genuinely moved by this."

When they had made these plans a few days ago they thought it would be mostly family and some pack. Some of the pack that had been there with them when it happened, but it seemed that the entire town had shown up, as well as members from other packs. Connor shifted on his seat again and reached for his mate. Still nothing.

He wanted to be with her. She hadn't woke much since they'd all left the mountain four days ago. She had been sleeping, thanks mostly to the drugs that Clint kept in her. But her injuries were massive and none of them had expected her to live, especially not him.

"She'll be fine. I know you want to be with her, but Mom wanted us all together." Connor looked at Austin as he spoke. "And you know how she gets when thing don't go her…"

They looked up when the woman they loved more than anything was brought in. Their mom was wheeled close to him and reached over him to pick up her spoon. She'd been holding onto it like a talisman since they left the mountain. She kissed his hand and spoke to him as she held it. "I talked to her when she was awake this morning and she said to keep you here even if I had to beat you on the head."

Connor nodded. He'd been told by Louise to come to this as well. He smiled when he thought of the argument they'd had before he'd left today…

"You're driving me insane. Go out, go somewhere." She was very weak and her voice was as well. When she reached for her water, he nearly fell over the chair to get it to her. "You see? Damn it, I can't get better if you keep watching over me like I'm some invalid. Go away."

"No. And you are an invalid. You were nearly killed a few days ago and I don't want anything else to happen to you." She growled and he had to fight the smile. He loved it when she got all feisty with him. "Why don't you just let me have my way with this and no one will get hurt?"

"Because as soon as I'm able, I'm going to hurt you." She closed her eyes and he watched as she drifted off again. He stood up, pulled her hand to his, and kissed it…

She'd saved them all. And had been nearly killed because of it. Phil had told him that had that ball of magic hit him, he would have been unable to prevent it from tearing through everyone in that room. As it was, the few wolves that it hit were all dead.

When she'd lunged at William, Connor thought his heart had stopped beating. She had been the most beautiful and frightening thing he'd ever seen. When she'd shifted in mid air like she had, he had been so shocked that he nearly didn't move himself out of harm's way. As it was, he had sustained minor injuries.

"Are you going to sit there all day or are you going to get up and say anything?" Austin nudged him hard in the ribs as he grinned at him. "Well?"

Connor looked around and realized that the service had begun.

"They want to know how your mate is," his mom told him softly. "Go up and tell them she's planning to kick your butt."

Connor nodded and went to the front of the large room. The casket, closed due to the fact that Timothy had done too much damage to himself to have it open, was covered in roses and greenery. The man had saved their mom and she had wanted this for him.

"I want first to thank you all for coming today. I know that none of you knew the man beside me, but he did save one of our own. If truth be known, he probably saved a great many more people that day as well by helping my mom contact us and have the man responsible taken out." Connor thought of his mate. "Louise is doing much better. She's very...stubborn and will more than likely fuss at you all for making such a big deal about her injuries."

"Sort of like she's been fussing at you?"

He laughed at the man's comment from the back of the room. It seemed to ease him somewhat. "Yes. She seems to think that she'll heal much faster if I leave her alone." The room seemed to relax a bit as he continued. "The man that was killed had murdered a great many people. More than the council had first thought. When she had figured out what he was they were able to subdue him for several minutes, but he got away from them. Had she not been there to waylay him there is no telling how much longer the council would have had to work on finding him."

They had told them that they needed to stick to the council killing William and not Louise. They had given several reasons, but the one that bothered him the most was because they didn't want to look as if they were incompetent. Which to Connor's family's way of thinking, they were. And it seemed to matter little to them that his brother and brother-in-law were head of the stupid thing.

He told the crowd that Louise would be at the next moon phase and thanked them again for helping them get his own home ready to be moved into. He sat down beside his mom before anyone could ask him any more questions.

"You did very well."

He looked at his mom and kissed her cheek.

"You should go home now and be with Lou…Louise. I think she will probably need someone to yell at soon."

He kissed her again and left. He was nearly all the way back to his brother's house when he decided to swing by the house they were building and see how much longer it was going to be. He was both surprised and impressed that it was looking like a house now instead of a shell of one.

"You were supposed to come home, not hang out at a construction site."

He smiled at her comment. Louise was getting pretty good at this mate thing.

"Are you?"

He frowned, thinking he'd missed something. *"Am I what, love?"* He walked back to his truck to go to her.

"Are you coming here? I know I've been a pain in the ass, but I miss you. And I have to pee. I thought I could make it

until you came back, but I can't really get up without hurting some. " He could feel her pain, but knew the moment she took it away from him. *"Do you suppose that we'll be able to not go to the trial?"*

The trial for her was next week. The entire council was going to be there, as well as some from other regions. Louise had saved a great many people, but she had killed a rare creature. Dragons were not as plentiful as they had once been.

"I'm pretty sure you have to be there." They both knew this. *"And Phil told you not to worry, and you know how he worries about everything."*

"Yes. I suppose." He heard her sadness, but before he could ask, she spoke again. *"If I'm asleep again, when you get here will you please just hold me? I know that you can do that, but nothing more, and I miss you."*

He promised her he would and drove the ten minutes to the house. When he got inside, she was indeed asleep and he stripped out of his suit and crawled into bed beside her. She didn't cuddle up like she had before, but simply touched him. He knew in that moment that she was going to be fine.

~~~

Louise hated being carried around, but today wasn't so bad. Connor held her like she was something precious and she loved it. They were headed to the dining room and it was her first trip out of the bedroom since she'd awakened there. He was nearly down the stairs when he stopped suddenly.

"You're whelping." His voice sounded like he was pissed and she tried to get away from him. "Don't. Don't move."

"If that means what I think it does, then yes. And if you call it that again, I'll hit you with the spoon your mom gave me. I forgot. I meant to tell you, but I forgot." She actually had thought she'd lost the baby until yesterday when she felt it move. "I was going to tell you."

"I should have known. I should have…you can't be that far along. Maybe a few days at most." She struggled again, and he sat on the step to hold her better. "What the hell are you doing? Do you want me to drop you both?"

"I didn't do it on purpose. The way we have sex all the time, it's small wonder that I'm not carrying fifty kids." She looked up at him with tears in her eyes. "I won't abort this thing. I never thought to have one of my own and now that I have it, I'm not getting—"

His kiss silenced her. She looked up at him when he lifted his head and she stared at him. He looked strange. Before she could ask him what was wrong he smiled at her.

"You can't abort our child, Louise, or I'll beat you senseless." He held her tightly to him. "I'm so happy, you've no idea."

"You're not mad at me?" He shook his head and she slapped him on the shoulder. "Then next time, don't yell at me when you ask something like that. Moron. I thought you were pissed off and now you tell me that you're happy."

"Do you two plan to join us so we can eat, or are you going to hang out on the stairs all night?"

She looked down at Austin who was leaning against the doorjamb. "There is enough food in this room right now that I'm reasonably sure we'll be eating leftovers for a month."

"We're whelping."

Lou slapped Connor again.

"We're going to have a baby. And Louise is excited to be having fifty of them."

"I am not. The things that come out of your mouth are…just take me to dinner. I'm not going to let your stupidity ruin my good mood about being out of that room with you." He stood up with her still in his arms and held her tight. "If you think I'll forget this then you're nutty as a fruitcake."

"I don't want you to forget that I love you and am thrilled beyond words to know that we're going to have a child."

She glanced down the stairs to see that Austin had left.

"He doesn't care if we come in now. He's probably wanting to tell them all, but won't. He'll leave that to us."

She nodded as the continued down the stairs. She had a great many questions to ask, mostly about the baby being alright, but she didn't. She wanted to be with his family and didn't want anyone to thinking she was stupid for thinking some of the things she was. When she was settled at the table Nancy kissed her cheek then leaned in and spoke to her.

"You told him then?"

Louise didn't even pretend to not know what she was referring to and nodded.

"Good. You're going to be fine once you move in and, if you ever need anything, all of us will be more than happy to help you. Especially with those questions that I'm sure are circling your head like a drain. Everything will be fine. You'll see."

Louise nodded, afraid of the answers she might get for her questions. Like what was the baby going to be? Would she have to teach it to shift? Too many for her to try to sort through right now.

They enjoyed the first course of soup. It was her favorite kind, potato cheese with ham and green onions. She was sitting back in her chair when Phil asked Nancy how she was doing.

"I'm fine. Just fine, as you know." She lifted her brow at him when he laughed. "What is it you think you know, young man?"

"I think you've been given something that has extended your life."

She stiffened beside her and Louise wanted to hurt the man at the other end of the table.

"Not me. I told you before that I wouldn't do that to you, but someone has."

"I don't know what you mean. I've been taking care of things here and not hanging out with other vampires. And so help me if you did this after I told you not to, I will—"

"I didn't. I swear to you."

Louise was confused and Phil must have known it.

"I have the power of life. And somehow Nancy figured it out and told me that if I gave her what I gave the rest of the family she would hurt me. I believed her. She told me that she missed her mate and I respected her wishes. But now I can see that…" He grinned.

"See what, you overgrown bug? Tell me what you think you know or, so help me, I will spoil that child of yours so badly that she'll only want her grandma at night and not either of you." Nancy was laughing, but Louise believed her. "Spill it before I do you."

"Did Timothy give you anything while he was with you?"

She nodded.

"I don't mean the key and other things, but anything…maybe liquid?"

"Yes. I told you he gave me some broth. But it wasn't tainted with anything. He took the first bite."

Phil nodded and smiled.

"Tell me or so help me, I will stake you."

"Why is that the first thing everyone wants to do when they get pissed at me?" He raised his hand. "It was dragon's blood. And Timothy had probably been taking it his entire life, all his lifetimes, so it wouldn't have done anything to him when he took the first bite."

Nancy looked around the room and then at Louise. She looked terrified and pissed. Her hand reached out and touched

Louise's cheek before settling on her lap again. Louise didn't know what she was going to say, but she was afraid too.

"Can you smell it on me?"

Louise looked around the room and her gaze settled back on Nancy.

"Can you smell the blood on me? You'd be the only one that would know for sure that…I don't want to live forever."

Louise leaned into her throat and took a deep breath. She smelled of home and comfort. She smelled of the earth and the sky, as well as an earthy smell she couldn't place. Just as she was pulling back to tell her she didn't smell anything, she caught it. The scent of the man she'd killed. "He's there. I'm so sorry."

Nancy nodded and put her arms around her.

"I'm so sorry you smell like me."

Nancy laughed. "I'm not. And I suppose if I must live beyond my years, it is better than with mosquito breath." She looked at Phil, then at the rest of her family. "I suppose this mean's I'll be babysitting for a lot longer than I thought."

She was sad. Louise was pretty sure that everyone at the table knew it too, but they laughed with her. Louise looked over at Connor, who nodded once at her and leaned back in his chair. He was leaving it up to her to tell her.

"I'm sort of glad you'll be around. Connor and I are going to have a baby or something too."

Nancy looked at her then at Connor.

"I thought that was what you were talking about when you were referring to moving into the house."

"Another baby?" Nancy put her hand on Louise's flat belly and closed her eyes. "Another child to hold. I never thought…" She brushed at the tears on her cheeks.

"Well maybe more than that. I think I'm in labor." Holly didn't move when she said that and neither did anyone else.

For several seconds. Then all hell broke loose, starting with the unflappable Phil.

"Labor? Now? You're in labor now?" Holly nodded and Louise laughed at Phil when he seemed to pale. "We have to do something. Christ, a baby. We're going to have a baby now."

"We will if you ever shut up and take me home." She stood and froze for several seconds then looked at her mom. "My water just broke."

Holly was picked up and rushed up the stairs. No more than her back hit the bed when she howled out in pain. Louise wasn't sure Phil could get any paler, but he did. She was ready to offer him her wrist when his mom came into the room and his father ushered him out. A few minutes later he came back in the bedroom a whole lot calmer.

Baby boy Campbell was brought into the world nine hours and ten minutes later. Holly was fine, as was the baby. Louise was thrilled beyond words that it appeared to be a regular-looking baby and not a wolf or bat. She flushed when Phil raised a brow at her and she wished once again he didn't have the ability to read her mind. She was nervous, damn it.

By the time everyone was settled she was exhausted and tried to make her way to her room so that Connor would be able to spend some time with his sister and new nephew. He scooped her up into his arms without a word and took her to the bedroom. She was asleep before she was under the covers.

CHAPTER 18

The house finished the next week. They still couldn't move into it yet as there was no furniture, but she was getting excited. Nancy had brought her the laptop yesterday to have her look at furniture. Tomorrow, she was going into town for three hours and she was going to do a lot of testing of cushions. And she was planning to seduce Connor.

The trial was the day after tomorrow and she was afraid. Phil had assured her in his weird way that she wouldn't be going to prison if she was convicted, but she would be put to death. Great.

"But not to worry. You have the best attorney known to all mankind at your side. As well as an in on the council." She wasn't amused and told him so. "They only want this to cover their own asses. They want to make sure you understand the importance of you keeping quiet on what actually happened there that day."

She'd been thinking about what had happened that day a great deal in the past few weeks. So much so that she didn't want to think about it again. She'd killed that man. Of course, he'd been trying to kill her and had indeed killed a great many others, but she had done the deed that had ended his life.

When he'd tried to get away she had not thought about the fact that she was much smaller than him and with a whole lot less magic, or whatever it was they shared. Her only thought had been if he got out of the place, he would reign terror down on her new family more than they could have thought of. She had only gone after him to stop him. Not to kill him.

Her wolf—she never thought of her as anything but a separate person—had been pissed. The man was getting away and she didn't like it. When Louise had jumped to stop him, the wolf inside of her had taken control.

The first time she'd bitten into him, she'd only gotten his shoulder. His blood was strong and tasted slightly bitter. She had pulled away and had been hit for her troubles. Her head had spun for several seconds, but she didn't stop. The wolf had attacked again, this time going for the soft of his belly.

Louise shuddered when she thought of how that had felt. Her teeth had touched through the softness and she had shaken her head to do more damage. His bowel had opened then and the smell, along with the taste, had made her gag. But he had gathered his magic and had touched her back with it. She cried out in so much pain that she'd let him go. He had laughed at them.

"You think to kill me? I think not, child. You cannot kill your creator."

She was hurting too badly by then to think about what he was saying until he asked her for the key.

"Give it to me and I will let you live. You see, I can kill you, but you cannot kill me."

The key. She'd had it around her neck when she'd shifted and could feel it touching her fur. She had no idea what it was for, but he did. She moved into his mind to find it, not realizing until Phil told her later that, as a wolf, she shouldn't have been able to do that.

It wasn't a key at all, but something that held all he was, he thought. She moved back and forth in front of him as he watched her, telling her that she was to obey him. Moving to the wall closest to them, she heard the others coming down that hall toward them. She knew as soon as she looked at him again that he was gathering whatever he could to kill them all as soon as the others got there.

It took her several seconds to get the chain off her neck. He smiled at her and held out his hand. She still wasn't sure if it was his good girl that pissed her off enough or simply that he thought she would do as he commanded. When she had it on the floor in front of her she picked it up gently with her mouth.

"Now, bring it to me and no one else will get hurt."

She started toward him and stopped just shy of him being able to touch her.

"Give it to me now and I'll kill you swiftly. If I have to come for it, then you'll suffer like you've never suffered before."

She saw it then. He was afraid she was going to break it. And if she did…he wasn't really sure what would happen, but he did know that he would die. Good enough reason for her. She bit it.

At first she hadn't been sure that she would be able to destroy it. It was hard and big in her jaws. Then when she dropped it, thinking to claw at it with her long nails, he'd sat up quickly and tried to snatch it from her. She'd grabbed it back up in her mouth just as he rolled over her and she rolled again until he was beneath her. She bit again, this time breaking it.

The scream was horrific. She knew at once that it was from him. But she was burning as well. Her mouth was on fire and she would feel the liquid, strangely dark and hot, drip from her canines. That's when she noticed him.

William was melting. His face where the liquid had touched him was gone, only bone was where his cheek had been. His eye was also gone and in its place was a hole deep into his skull that was as dark as the night. She started to move off him, but he had grabbed her and his fingers now tangled in her fur. Whimpering once, she looked up when someone touched her from above.

"Let him go."

She didn't know the man in front of her, not even when he knelt down to her level.

"Let the key go and he will no longer hold onto you." He touched her again and she could hear the others coming. He looked to the door before he looked at her again. "They cannot find me here with you. This is my last good deed before I go to the place all bad people go to."

The connection to this man was quick. She could see that he was the man who had saved Nancy. "No. You will not. We owe you so much."

He smiled when she released the key and it fell right into William's mouth. When it did he jerked several times before she was tossed off him and against the far wall. The change was amazing.

He was first a dragon. Big and dark, she could see how he would have been a large creature. But he changed again and again, each time getting darker and uglier. Every time he would shift he became so far from what he'd been born as, into something that no longer existed. Then he simply stopped. He lay there as a man, whole and unharmed. But dead nonetheless. She looked over at Timothy when he stood up. The others were spilling into the room as he stood there.

"You have done something no others could have done." He looked at the man lying there so still. "He was once a great man, wonderful to all mankind, but he became bitter and greedy. You are nothing like him."

Then he disappeared and she closed her eyes.

"Are you all right?" She hadn't realized that she had fallen asleep until she heard Connor's voice. "You looked like you were having a nightmare. Were you?"

"No. Just thinking about what had happened." She had told him everything, as well as Phil. "Come here and lay down with me."

"No. If I do then I won't be able to stay awake. I've been working to get the house done, as well as a few orders that I completely forgot about." He stretched and she felt her body respond. He stopped and looked at her. "You keep smelling like that and I won't ever get my orders finished. I've only come here to get a quick bite to eat and a shower. Behave."

She let her need for him wash over her. She knew he would smell her; she could as well. Moving to the edge of the bed, she let the sheet pool in her lap. The t-shirt she had on didn't hide very much.

"It's been a long time, Connor, and I want you." She was not going to pussy foot around any longer and wait for him to come to her. She started to stand up and stopped when he moved toward her. "You come to bed with me now and I'll make it worth your while."

He hesitated and she wanted to scream at him. "The doctor said to wait for another few days. I'm not going to be able to if you keep that up."

She didn't want him to. She stood up then and walked toward him, taking off her shirt as she went. This time, she was going to get him to make love to her even if it killed her. Or her him. Whichever, she was getting him naked.

"Stop."

She did. She wasn't sure what he wanted, but didn't move.

"It's my turn. You had your way with me the last time, now it's my turn."

"What is it you want to do to me, Connor? Because from where I'm standing, you're entirely too dressed and way too far away." When he pulled his shirt over his head and dropped it to the floor, her mouth watered. "Connor, are you going to make love to me or is this a ploy to get me to go back to bed?"

"Oh you'll be going back to bed, soon, and me with you, but first I want to shower with you. I've only just realized that I've not been able to wash that lovely red hair of yours. That amazing body hasn't had me go over it with a soapy sponge, and I've not had the ultimate pleasure of taking you against the wall while the water beats down on us."

Her knees trembled.

"Don't fall now. If you do then I won't be able to do all the things I've been thinking about for the past month."

"You've thought of me?" She knew that she sounded pleased, but didn't care. He'd been thinking about her. He nodded as he moved again. "In what way?"

"Mostly beneath me. Also when you're over me, riding me. I love watching your face when you're enjoying yourself." This time when he moved he stopped just short of touching her. "But I simply love you. And no matter what we do, I will enjoy it."

He took her mouth in the gentlest kiss she'd ever gotten. As he touched her it was like he was touching her soul. When Connor lifted his head he looked down at her and she knew, for as long as she lived, the look on his face would remind her of how much she loved him. Kissing him again, she led him to the bathroom.

~~~

Connor walked behind her, knowing that he was going to make love to her all night. Smiling, he thought of what Clint had told him just that morning. He wondered what the man would do when faced with the lovely creature he'd walked in on.

"If you have to, stay away from the bedroom. She needs to rest, not romp in the sack with you."

Connor had lifted his brow at the man's old fashion terminology.

"She's just gone through more than most wolves go through in their entire lives. She did it all in one day. Stay out of the bedroom."

Who was he to say no to his mate? Certainly not him. And certainly not when she was doing all the things he'd been thinking about for weeks. Years even. He wanted her in the worst way.

As she turned on the water to the shower he stopped her. He wanted to bathe with her in a nice, deep, warm tub. He'd had a very nice one installed in their bathroom so that they could have as much fun as they wanted and not soak the lower floors. He told her what he wanted. "You wait and I'll take care of this." He picked her up and sat her on the counter. "I want this to be perfect."

"It is, so long as you're here."

He grinned.

"I mean it. I don't need all this fancy stuff. I just want you."

Connor kissed her nose and went to find the lighter that CJ had given him a week ago to light some pretty candles for Lou. He was lighting the third one when he thought of music. Hurrying out of the bathroom, he turned on the radio only to be blasted by the hard rock he had been listening to over a month ago. Turning it to something soft and sexy, he went back to the bath.

"I thought I could help." She'd finished off the dozen candles for him. "Connor, please. I seriously don't need all this romance. Sex is fine without it."

"Yes, but I don't want fine. I want romantic. I want you to blush when you think of the trouble I went to. I want you to…" He sat her on the counter again. "I want you to sit here like a good girl and leave me to my work." He swatted her ass and moved back to his job. The candles were a nice soft vanilla scent and he hoped she liked them. When she spoke behind him he nearly dropped the lighter.

"You have the cutest butt. Has anyone ever told you that?"

He shook his head, trying his best to concentrate on what he was doing. He did moan when she cupped her hands over his ass cheeks and squeezed.

"They're hard as stone too. And a nice size."

He nearly swallowed his tongue when she reached between his legs and cupped his balls. He didn't move when she moved up his shaft to the tip and then back down again. He knew what she was doing. She was seducing him and he didn't have the strength to stop her. When he started to turn to her, she stopped him.

"No. I want to touch you. Feel you." He set the lighter on the window ledge and held onto the tub with both hands. He hoped to Christ that he didn't fall and kill himself because there was no blood in his head. "You have nice hips. They aren't like some people's, but make a nice flare from your rock hard abs to them. I guess it has to do with running all the time."

"It's in our DNA to be slim. I suppose it has to do with being hunters to survive." He felt her press her body to his and he moaned. "Louise, you're supposed to be sitting down and letting me have you."

"I know, but you looked so yummy like this that I just wanted a small taste." Her teeth bit his shoulder and he had to grip the side of the tub harder. He was going to leave fingerprints, he knew it. "Did you know that you taste like muscle to me? I know that sounds stupid, but the way you feel when I bite you makes me think of big, strong men and muscles."

He groaned again. "I need to protect you. And if you don't stop that right now, someone is going to get hurt." Her laughter made him smile.

"You won't hurt me. Not on purpose anyway." She ground herself against his ass and he reached out his left hand and pulled her flush against him. "You like that? You like me touching you like this?"

Her voice got huskier, almost primal. He wanted to stand and turn, but also wanted this to build. When she ground herself against him again, he did stand this time and leaned against the wall. She ran her hands up his chest and pulled none too gently on his nipples. When her fingers trailed down his chest, he sucked in his belly when she reached into his pants.

His cock, already hard, seemed to stretch out for her. She ran her thumb over the tip and he knew when her hand disappeared, she was licking it clean. Connor turned to watch her. Her hand was just about to enter her mouth and he grabbed her. "You want to taste me? All of me?"

She nodded and dropped to her knees before him. He said, "Water," and she turned it off before coming back to him. She had his pants undone in seconds. His cock out in less time than that. She was poised to take him into her mouth when she looked up at him. "Will you please come down my throat?"

He could only nod at her.

"And if I don't do this right, will you let me know?"

She had to be kidding. He looked hard to see if she was teasing him and couldn't see anything but fear. She really did think she was going to be bad at this. He cupped the back of her head and pulled her to him. "Take me in your mouth and run your tongue over me. Do what you want, only be careful of your teeth. I'm sort of sensitive down there." She fit her mouth over his head and he nearly fainted with pleasure.

After several minutes of this, he was sure she'd been trained by the most talented courtesans. He felt his eyes roll to the back of his head and he didn't even care that he was begging her to never stop. When she cupped his balls Connor couldn't help it; he cried out his release and jettisoned deep down the back of her throat. He nearly came off the floor when she took one of his balls into her mouth.

Breathing hard, he pulled her away. She looked hungry and needy. Her scent perfumed the air in the room and he felt his sated cock stir. "Counter. Get on the counter." She only stared at him. He knew just how she felt. Dazed and confused, he repeated what he wanted her to do. By the time he got his pants off completely, she was just sitting on the edge.

It was his turn. He knew that she was close; hell, he was as well, so he slid two of his fingers into her sheath even with her panties still on. He watched her lean back and spread her thighs.

"I'm going to make you come fast and hard. Then I'm going to lean you over that sink and fuck you until neither of us can walk." She moaned and reached for her breast. "Louise, I think maybe I might die from this."

"We'll go together. And it'll be sooner rather than later." She continued her journey of exploring her breast and nipple. "Connor, please do something. I'm so close to coming I think my head might explode."

He stood up knowing that after this, he was done. But, hell, what a way to go. Tearing her panties off, he slammed into her deep. Her body not only accepted him, but seemed to take more of him into her. Even as he pulled out to the tip, he could feel her climax skirting over the edge. When he sank himself home he took her mouth and captured her screams of release.

Connor came again. Not hard, not even enough to drain him much more. But he was drained. As much as he'd been if he'd run a marathon. He doubted if the house caught on fire he'd be able to make it out alive. He had nothing left. When she giggled he lifted his head with the last his strength. "And you laugh now why?" She giggled again and he lifted her chin to kiss her quickly and ask if she was all right.

"Yes, but I never got my bath and neither did you." Connor accepted her kiss. "But now I'm exhausted. Do you think you can still take me to bed?"

Her yawn was what got him and he yawned as well. Lifting her up, he took her to the bedroom, glad it was only a few feet away, and dropped her onto it. When she scrambled under the covers he walked to the other side and joined her. As soon as her head lay on his chest, he knew she was asleep. He joined her a few minutes later, smiling hugely at his good fortune.

CHAPTER 19

The trial was a mess and it hadn't even begun yet. There were perhaps a thousand people outside the large conference building and at least half that inside. There was not only nowhere to sit, but there was barely enough room to stand. Louise watched the people come and go as she sat with Phil. He looked so calm she wanted to smack him.

"Am I going to be put to death?"

He glanced over at her, pulling his eyes away from his son and wife for a few seconds. When he looked lost, she repeated her question.

"Probably not. They need this trial to make sure that what you did doesn't come back to bite them in the ass. I would say that it'll be over with by the end of the week. Maybe Wednesday of the next week, but no more." She groaned at his prediction. "You think it'll go longer?"

"Christ, I hope not. I just want this stupid thing over with." She looked up when he did. "Is that the judge?"

"Yes. Beautiful, isn't she? My mom had been presiding over these things since well before I was born." She looked at Hope like she was a lifeline. "But don't expect her to cut you any slack because she's my mom. She'll more than likely be harder on you because of it."

Great. The mom of her attorney. Just what she didn't need. But she didn't say anything more, couldn't really. Mrs. Campbell as well as Phil were going at it. There was some concern on his part about there being too many people near his child.

"There is any number of germs in this room and now they're breathing all over him."

Lou wanted to pick up the nearest object, preferably a wooden stake, and stab him to death with it. He winked at her when she tugged at his pristine white shirt. "What the hell are you doing? Don't antagonize the judge, please." She picked up his briefcase. "If you don't stop this right now, I'm going to beat you to death with this."

He took it from her and set it on the other side of him. She couldn't reach it without walking around the table. He sat down and cocked a brow at her when she didn't join him right away. "I'm softening her up."

Lou looked at the judge then back at Phil and raised her own brow.

"I am. She loves the baby and will hurry this along so that he doesn't catch anything now."

"So you just expedited my trial in the name of your kid's well being. Awesome. Now I get to be shot sooner."

Phil started shaking his head.

"No what, you dickweed?"

"No, you won't be shot. They behead beings that kill their own kind." He stood up again when Hope asked who wanted to begin.

She was ten minutes into the trial when what he said occurred to her. As soon as he said it, he had called her to the stand and she was asked to give her life if it was later found out that she had lied. She agreed to that too, apparently, because she was sitting in the big chair next to the dais.

"Did you say I would be beheaded?" Her voice cracked and squeaked. "Like they take off my head?"

Louise flushed when the courtroom laughed. She was nearly ready to crawl under the table, any table as a matter of fact, that she nearly missed what was being said. She looked over at Phil when he cleared his throat.

"She wants to know if you're finished with your narrative of the events."

Louise nodded then shouted that she wasn't. "That man? The one I killed? He was going to rape me with a machine and take out my eggs. He didn't care that I might have use for them later. Now, as a matter of fact, but he wanted them and damn the consequences." She flushed again. "Sorry. But he was going to kill me if I didn't kill him first. And you know that he was responsible for that poor Timothy's death even if he didn't actually pull the trigger."

Phil winked at her and she was sure that she would, at this very moment murder him as well. When he turned to the judge, his mom, she looked ready to burst into tears or laughter. Lou wasn't sure which and was sure she didn't want to know. When she stood up, she was asked to have a seat. They weren't quite finished yet. The other man stood up and glared at Phil when he said something low to the other man. This man made Phil look like a dwarf in comparison and Phil was not a little man.

"Miss Cavanaugh, I just have a few questions for—"

"It's Force. Louise Force. And if you want me to answer you, you'll remember that." She looked at Hope when she cleared her throat. "He knows damn good and well who I am. He just met me in the back room not an hour ago."

"You met with my client?" The room seemed poised on something. Phil stood up and asked the other man once again if he had met her. When he didn't answer, he looked at her.

"What is it he wanted? What did he ask you without your lawyer present?"

Louise thought there was a trap here, but didn't know whose side it was going to come from. She looked at the man in question and saw him pale then shake his head just a little. He wanted her to lie to her own fucking lawyer.

Tell me the truth and I swear to you that this will end well for you. I don't care what it is, even if he asked you where the fucking bathroom was.

She glanced at Phil, suddenly glad for the connection. *"I'm not in trouble?"*

Phil told her no she wasn't.

"Mr. Simpson asked me if I was sure that the key was for nothing more than to kill William with. He asked me if I had tried to find an alternative usage for it or simply used it as a murder weapon." She looked at Hope then at Phil. "He seemed to think that the key was to something of monetary value."

"Was it?"

She looked at Hope when she asked. Her tone indicated that she already knew the answer. Louise shook her head. "William didn't know what the key was for. He hadn't seen it before that night. Timothy had it all this time." She looked at Mr. Simpson. "That man said that it was the key to everything. I suppose it was. For me at least."

"And what do you mean he didn't know what the key was for? He was afraid of it, you had said." Phil picked up a file and opened it. "You wrote in your own words that 'William looked at the key like he knew what it was, but I didn't think he'd ever actually seen it.' So you believe he knew of it, but had not seen it."

Louise looked around the room and felt Phil whisper through her mind to just tell the truth. She nodded once and decided that it was now or never. These people would either accept her for what she was or she'd be beheaded. She looked right at Connor as she continued her story. "He didn't know what it was for, only what he'd been told it could do to him. It was supposed to either make him stronger if he held it, or kill him if someone else had it, or so he'd been told when he found out there was a key. I made him believe it was much more than that." She shifted on her seat. "I slipped into his mind and had him believe that once it was broken over him that it would melt away his skin until he was nothing left but bone. He…I guess he believed me."

"So it was just a simple key."

Louise shook her head.

"Then what? It's useless now that you've broken it. No one will ever know what it was supposed to be used for or if he had millions hidden away and locked with that key." The other attorney flushed when Hope banged her gavel down. "I'm just trying to get to the real reason the key might have been used."

He sat down and Louise tried her best not to look at Nancy. She had been with her every day since that day and they had talked endlessly. She looked over at Hope when Mr. Simpson sat down and huffed.

"Do you have anything else to add to this? Or are you going to sulk like a small child?" Hope smiled when he glared at them both. "I see. Well then I happily order these proceedings over. Louise Force, you are free to go." Everyone stood up, including Mr. Simpson. "Not so fast, Billy Simpson. You have some explaining to do. Some of which has to do with you contacting Mrs. Force here without her council."

Louise heard him sound as if he was beginning to complain, but she tuned him out. Her family, all of them, were pulling her in for a group hug. And what a hug it was.

~~~

"What happened to the key?" Connor looked at Phil before looking at Louise. "You do know that had he asked you if you had it, you would have had no choice but to tell him? It's the reason we hold these things in that building. It's been enhanced with magic."

"There was no key. Remember, it was broken." Connor didn't like the look that his mom and Louise exchanged. Nor the look of satisfaction that Phil had on his face. "What happened?"

Louise took out the key and the map and laid them on the table. She didn't say anything, but glanced over at his mom. There was something so wrong about the look she had on her face.

"I didn't tell anyone, not even Louise, until later. I didn't know what made me do it, but... Well, I didn't give her the right key. The one I gave her was on Timothy's body when we found him." She reached out and touched the map then picked up the key. "I found this one in the first aid kit that Timothy left me. The map was in it too."

"What if the key hadn't killed him? What if the...Christ." Connor sat down hard when he thought of all the things that could have gone wrong. His mother hit him with her wooden spoon and he wanted to growl at her. He might have too if she wasn't so fucking mean about it.

"You behave. Of course it would kill him. That's why it was laying out there for everyone to see when we found poor Timothy's body. He certainly didn't have it out like that when we were together." She huffed at him again and went to stand by the sink to finish up the potatoes for dinner. "That poor man gave me what he knew I'd use. He'd already given me the map. The key would have been useless without it killing William and he knew it."

Connor wasn't sure when she'd lost him, but he realized that he didn't have a clue what the hell she was talking about. He eyed the spoon in her apron pocket and wonder if he could get it from her without being brain damaged before he could get away. She turned to look at him as if she knew what he was thinking. He said the first thing he could think of, hoping she wouldn't call him on the spoon. Or hit him with it.

"And you two, what have you done with this map and key? Gone out spelunking? Or have you been scouring the mountain looking for the lost treasure?" He flushed. He'd been nasty, but he was also a little pissed. She'd not told him.

"We've done both, thanks." She sat next to him and he picked her up and put her on his lap. "We found something, but…but not anything of value to anyone but me, I guess. The world too if I were to let it go, but I won't. Not ever."

"It's the formulas he used." His mom put the big notebook on the table with a smallish box. "I took some of the pages to the university and asked them to look them over. Not a lot, mind you, but just snippets of a page here and a page there. They said it was the work of a mad man. A man who needed to be locked up."

Connor picked up the book and thumbed through some of the pages. There were pictures, crude ones that showed Louise as a child. A layout of a lab and a list of things needed in one. There was a longer list on another page that had the same things on it, but some had been crossed out and other things added. There were prices of some of the equipment and a list of people he wanted to work for him. He laughed when he saw the name of a very famous chemist. One who had been dead a very long time.

"So, you have the inner workings of a madman. Now what? I know you said you won't use it. But something has to be done with this information." He looked at Louise when she put the book back on the table and handed him the box. "What's this? Another key?"

"It's my birth certificate." He took out the topmost sheet of paper and opened it. She took it from him and pointed to the top. "It's my real name. The one they gave me in the lab."

"Eve Cinderella Cavanaugh." He looked at the name of her parents. "Someone decided to call you after your mother. Her name was Ginger Louise Spatter. William James Bond is listed for your father."

He watched her fold the sheet back out and take out another. "This is the list of 'donors' that they put into my test-tube. I think they wanted to keep it all straight. All of them are in that box, or at least their pictures are. They all had a…all those men were a part of my life the entire time I was a child. The pool guy." She handed him a picture. Then another. "That guy was our door man. This guy was the first foster family I stayed with when I was forced out of the orphanage."

"They kept tabs on you."

She nodded.

"At least until you ran away from Herman. Then they must have lost track of you."

"It's in there as well. The ramblings of William. He had a list of these men and they were marked off with dates. I'm assuming either when he killed them or asked them where I was." She handed him a neatly typed up sheet. "Your mom made a list of them and she checked on them at the library. All of them died a horrific death."

Connor watched her put everything back in the box and close the lid. He knew she was upset. Could even understand it. But what he didn't understand was how to help her. But he did love her.

"There are some things you should be aware of. Things that now that we have this, it makes things a bit easier for you." Phil sat down and pulled out a file. "Your…whatever you want to call him claimed you on the birth certificate, so you are entitled to all his—"

"I don't want anything of his." She stiffened in his arms and he held her tightly. "You do whatever you want with it. I don't want to have a thing to do with it."

Phil nodded. "I can understand your not wanting his things, but there is a matter of his money. There is a great deal of it."

"I don't care."

Connor didn't let her go when she started to cry.

"He tried to do things to me that…you have to know that he was nothing more than a man who I knew."

"I can do what you want with it, but I'd like to make a suggestion."

Louise nodded.

"Austin has a large pack here, a pack that you're now a part of. There are over seventy children here that will need help with educational needs, college. Some of them might be in need of housing help during college. What if I set up a foundation to help defray the costs to help the pack? No one would ever know where it came from."

She looked at Connor and he nodded. Louise looked back at Phil and he smiled. "I have things I'd like to make clear. Things about the money. It can't be used for what he was doing. I don't care if someone uses it to go to college and do research, but they can't set up a lab somewhere and start doing what William was doing."

"I can make that happen." He pulled out a sheet of paper and started making notes. "How about you think of a name for it? A name that will reflect what you want the money used for."

He started to tell her to take her time in thinking about that when she spoke again. "The Timothy Bennett Foundation. Isn't that what you found his last name was?"

"Yes. Yes, it was." After making a few more notes, he stood up. "I have to go and take care of Holly. She and the baby were going to watch television when I left."

After a few minutes everyone left them in the kitchen and Connor simply held her. She seemed to be the most relaxed he'd seen her in a long while. He kissed her shoulder and stood up with her in his arms. It was really late and they were going to move into their new home tomorrow.

"Connor? Let's go to our house. Let's become wolves and run over there right now and sleep in our new bed. Tonight."

He liked the idea. "I don't think you should plan on doing much sleeping, love. I have plans of breaking in that bed of ours. What do you think of that?"

Her answer nearly had him fall over. She nuzzled her face into his neck and nipped at his flesh. A soft moan from her about had him tossing her over his shoulder, taking her upstairs and fucking, but her next words made him change his mind.

"If you take me to the house, I'll let you tie me up."

Connor took them outside and put her down. "Hurry. Hurry before I take you right here on the porch." He loved her giggle and smiled as he watched her strip. He almost forgot what he was doing he was so mesmerized by her skin being revealed to him, inch by inch.

CHAPTER 20

The run was fantastic. They had both shifted and she couldn't seem to run fast enough or long enough through the woods. She loved the way she felt and the way things smelled. Sharper, much earthier. She had just come out from behind a large bush when he jumped her, knocking her to the ground.

"I need you," he growled through her mind. *"I need to bury myself deep in you while you're a wolf."*

"Yes." Her body was ready for him in that second. But she wanted to be chased by him, dominated by him. Louise took off running and didn't stop even when she felt him getting close. Didn't slow when she knew that it was only a matter of seconds before he took her to the ground.

When it happened she'd thought she was prepared, but his heavy body had rolled her over and over until she was beneath him. His larger body, muscled and strong, held her down to the ground without any problems. She whimpered when he bit her hard on the shoulder.

"My beast wants you and he'll have you."

She wanted to tell him yes again but didn't.

"You ran from us. You can't run from us when you smell like sex to us."

She curled her body up and rubbed herself under him. When he bit her again, she nearly came. Then he dropped his weight over her and she was lying flat on the ground.

"Lay still. If you move again, I'm not going to be able to be gentle with you. I want to, but fuck, you're driving me insane." She moved again and felt his cock. *"You are still a virgin in this body. If I take you, it's going to hurt."*

"Hurt me, Connor, please. I need to feel you take me this way." He shifted over her, but didn't let her up. She wanted to run again, but knew that if she tried again he'd really hurt her.

When he mounted her from behind, she nearly cried out when he slammed deep inside of her. His cock was thicker than she'd thought it would be and much longer. She waited for him to move and when he didn't, she did. His canines sank deep in her shoulder.

He held her down as he took her. He moved so quickly that she couldn't seem to get a grasp on his rhythm and build up to a climax as well. And that alone made her see stars. When he put his paws on her back and pushed her down more, she knew that he was close to coming. Knew that she too was going to come with him.

"Christ, I need you." His breath was hot on her muzzle and she realized she could move more. *"Come with me, baby. Come now."*

She did. Her body came apart and seemed to put itself back together again before she did it again. When Connor stiffened behind her, he bit her again, this time hard, and she knew that it was different somehow. But when he howled, her body hard and jerking behind when he did it, she knew that he had come as well.

~~~

They had shifted an hour ago. Both of them relaxed enough not to care about the stones biting into neither their backsides nor the occasional bug that landed on them. She rolled over and rested her head on his chest and looked at him. His eyes were closed, but she knew he was awake.

"How long do you think it will be before we don't want to have sex any longer?"

He raised his head and looked at her for a second before he dropped back down and closed his eyes. "Never. Where do you come up with this stuff?" He rolled her to her back quickly. "Or do you need for me to prove it to you again how much I love your body?"

His body was hard and she felt his cock stir on her thigh. She reached up, pulled his head to hers, and kissed him. They both deepened the kiss and after several seconds, Connor made his way down her body to her breasts and worried her nipple. "I love the way you taste. Especially after sex. You're salty and hot." His tongue seemed to glide over her skin, leaving a hot trail behind it. "There is nothing I'd like better than to take you again, but I don't want to injure either of us by doing it on the ground. Let's go home."

After dressing, they walked over to the new house. It was lovely even in the twilight. He asked her what she wanted to do first after they woke up in the morning.

"I should find a job." She looked at him when he laughed. "I'm serious. I have never not made my way in the world." She knew he was aware of her last few years. They'd talked about her being homeless and how she'd ended up at the Force compound. And she thought he was all right with it. She looked over at him as they opened the door to the house. He stopped her before they went inside.

"Going through this door is a new beginning for us. Once we cross over the threshold, nothing that happened before matters and everything from now on does." He picked her up in his arms and held her to him. "Today, we start our lives together. No matter what, I will always love you more than myself and cherish you longer than either of us will live. And the child you now carry will know nothing but love, understanding, and that his or her parents would do anything for them. Do you understand?"

"Yes. You love me. As much as I love you."

~~~

Myles watched them go inside before he moved out from behind the tree. He'd been walking the woods when he'd heard them coming toward him and, rather than make himself known, he simply pulled the shadows around him and stood still. He really liked the couple and hoped they had a long life together. He walked in the opposite direction of both the pack house as well as the home behind him.

He was depressed. He knew that it was stupid to feel that way after all he'd been given since he'd meet the Forces and the Campbells, but he was, damn it. There were very few beings who could lay claim to the fact that they'd died and woke up a new man. Completely. Myles looked up at the night sky.

He'd been a vampire for nearly a whole year now. A whole year since his life had been ripped from him in a clothing store. He wasn't mad at Phil for doing what he'd done. He might have done the same thing had things been different. But to be able to live forever... Well, Myles was still trying to wrap his head around that.

When his cell phone rang he didn't even pull it out to see who it was. He didn't want to talk to anyone right now. Taking a few more steps, he heard the voicemail chime and again ignored it. He needed to get his head on straight before he could even consider talking.

Phil had told him to go and find himself. The man had even offered him one of his many homes to stay in. Then told him to go and stay in all of them. The flight plan for the jet was still sitting on his bedside table at home. There were even two credit cards brimming with cash on them and enough clothes in his closet to wear something new every day.

But he didn't want to leave just yet.

He hadn't fed yet. Oh, he thought, he'd eaten. There wasn't anything he couldn't eat now that he couldn't before. The tastes were even richer and more plentiful, but nothing made him go all stupid like his first dark beer had or his first taste of really dark chocolate. But he hadn't drunk from another person. And wasn't sure he would ever be able to.

His phone rang again then, when it stopped, it rang almost immediately again. He pulled it out to frown at the number. He didn't recognize it and answered to tell the prick to stop fucking calling him if he didn't answer. He had his mouth opened to do just that when the woman on the other end laughed.

"Hello, big boy. How's it hanging? Found yourself a beautiful woman to spend those lonely nights with?"

He stopped walking and sat down. This was the fourth time she'd called him in the year he'd been changed. The author friend of Phil's. "No. I'm still waiting for you to do that with. All those long and wonderfully sweaty nights with just you, me, and some silk sheets." Myles didn't own silk sheets, but for her, he'd go out and knit them, or whatever you did to make them, just for her. He had to adjust his cock twice when she laughed. It was throaty and warm. He thought of summer showers and hot, sex-filled nights when he heard it.

"You're so bad." The purr he loved as well spilled over the lines. "I have a problem with one of my books and was wondering if you could help a poor writer's-blocked friend."

"Anything. Is it a sex scene you need me to come over and act out with you? Or maybe you want me to pose for one of your covers. Some of them are enough to steam off the words on the other side."

She called him a charmer and laughed. "No, what I have is a technical question. And if you help me, I'll dedicate the book to you. What do you say, big boy? Wanna come and play with me?"

He nearly whimpered, but he just caught himself. Clearing his throat, he had to remember that they'd been playing this game every time she called him. Only today, he wasn't going to bail on her. "You tell me where to come to and I'll be in Phil's plane so quickly that I'll be there before you can type the next sentence." He'd never met her and was now up and walking toward where he'd parked his car. "I can be very helpful to beautiful women when they need me technically."

"I'm living in Paris right now, but I'm going home tonight. You come to my house in Ohio and we'll collaborate on the book." Laughter again. "We might be able to collaborate on a few other things while you're here."

He was nearly to his apartment when he hung up. Ten minutes later, he was making his way to the airport and the already fueled up jet. He was out of here as soon as he could manage it.

Myles had been reading her books for months. Every time another one came out, he would devour it for vampire information. No one knew the author was a real, live vamp, but he did. And while he was sitting on the runway he pulled out her latest book and started to read the next chapter.

When Al woke in a hospital bed, the first thing she noticed was the pain. As soon as she opened her eyes, the entire nightmare of what had happened since they got out of the car came crashing back like a slow-moving horror movie. The stalker, her father, brother, and Diana, the wolves hurting and killing them, everything in slow-moving pictures. Her screams ripped from her, one right after the other until someone came in and stabbed her with something sharp and she was drifting back into the blackness.

The next time she woke, she used the few seconds between reality and the nightmares to get a good grip on herself and try to control the urge to scream again. She barely managed to hold on, and only moaned this time. She looked around the room, and noticed that she wasn't alone. A woman in a hospital security uniform sat in a chair next to the bed. They stared at each other for several seconds before she spoke to Al.

"Jak se cítíš slečno Můžu ti něco přinést ?"

Al knew enough Czech to get her a room and a cab before this happened, maybe. Now she understood the woman perfectly. She wanted to know if she was alright and if she wanted anything.

"I'm fine, and no thank you. Do you know where Diana Lake is?" She didn't have to wonder if she was speaking correctly to her in her own language, Al just knew that she was speaking to her, and she understood. She was suddenly very scared.

"Ano , ano . slečno Lakeová . Já ji dostanu ." She said that she was going to get Diana, get her. Maybe she wasn't hurt after all; maybe it was a bad dream after all.

While Al waited, she looked around the room again. It was the basic hospital room, she guessed. Pretty wallpaper with floral prints on them. There was in addition to the chair the guard had been in, a couch. The equipment, with the exception of the IV stand, had been pushed back against the far wall. The television was on but muted, and closed captions ran across the bottom of the screen. The bed was wider than the ones her mother had been in, and the sheets where pink instead of the standard white.

Her body didn't hurt so much anymore. Lifting her arms up to inspect them, she noticed that other than the IV needle still in place on the back of her hand, she didn't have a mark on her. Gingerly running her hand down her waist, she didn't feel any wound there either, not even a bandage. She reached up and touched her mouth and found her lips to be smooth and soft, not broken and dry like they had been in the cave. Shaking now, she pulled the tray across the bed, opened the little drawer beneath it, and flipped up the mirror. Nothing. Not a single bruise.

Several minutes later, after the guard had left the room, Diana burst into it, rushed to her bed, and launched herself into her arms. Al had never been so happy to see anyone in her entire life.

"I thought you were dead. We all did. They had to bring in this special tracker to find you. When they found you in that cave the police actually thought you might already be dead. She said that it would take someone very strong to survive what you probably went through. I told her that you were the strongest person I knew and you'd be fine. And you are."

Al looked at Diana and thought she wasn't strong at all and, if given half a chance, she'd hire that tracker to take her back to the cave and leave her there. "I wish she had left me there. What about Dad and Jacob? Please tell me that they are alright too. That this whole thing was just a bad dream." She knew that they weren't. She could still see her father's intestines being ripped out and eaten by that...that thing. Jacob...she didn't want to think about the horrors her little brother had endured before he died. But she had little hope that any of it was a dream or, in this case, a nightmare.

"Oh Miss Bennett, they're both dead. I'm so sorry. I thought you knew. They both were killed immediately." Diana

looked away from her. She knew something, Al thought. She was hiding something from her.

"What is it Diana? What aren't you telling me? There's something else, isn't there? What is it?" She was ready to run, to run back to where they'd found her and hide. She knew whatever she had to tell her, she wasn't going to like it.

"Those animals, the ones that attacked us, they bit you to the point of almost death. That woman, Bailey, said that they infect people that way, with their bites. They were wolves, you see, werewolves. And now that you've been bitten by them, there's a very good possibility that you might become a werewolf too."

ABOUT THE AUTHOR

Kathi Barton, author of the bestselling series Force of Nature, lives in Nashport, Ohio with her husband Paul. In addition to writing full time Kathi likes to spend time with her eight grandkids, three children and three children-in-laws. She writes to relax and have fun.

Her muse, a cross between Jimmy Stewart and Hugh Jackman brings them to life for her readers in a way that has them coming back time and again for more. Her favorite genre is paranormal romance with a great deal of spice. You can visit Kathi on line and drop her an email if you'd like. She loves hearing from her fans. aaronskiss@gmail.com.

Follow Kathi on her blog:
http://kathisbartonauthor.blogspot.com/